"Even without the trench coat, you're perfect," Hannah said.

Dan thought that Sam Spade would have described her voice as whisky smooth and just as addictive.

"Perfect, even down to the five-o'clock shadow." She took his arm

It didn't take Hannah but a moment to understand that the steely look in his eyes meant *whoa*, not thanks for the compliment.

But when a reporter called out his name, Hannah's hunk put a crooked smile on his lips that didn't match the hardness in his gaze or the tightness of his muscles as he drew her into his arms. Before she could protest, he lowered his head and captured her lips.

Hannah was so shocked that it took her a moment to realize she was not just being kissed, but caressed, fondled, groped, mauled by a stranger whose touch turned her knees to soggy pasta. She tried to pull away.

"Please," he murmured. "Get me away from here and I'll do anything you want . . . ."

WHAT ARE *LOVESWEPT* ROMANCES?

They are stories of true romance and touching emotion. We believe those two very important ingredients are constants in our highly sensual and very believable stories in the *LOVESWEPT* line. Our goal is to give you, the reader, stories of consistently high quality that may sometimes make you laugh, sometimes make you cry, but are always fresh and creative and contain many delightful surprises within their pages.

Most romance fans read an enormous number of books. Those they truly love, they keep. Others may be traded with friends and soon forgotten. We hope that each *LOVESWEPT* romance will be a treasure—a "keeper." We will always try to publish

LOVE STORIES YOU'LL NEVER FORGET
BY AUTHORS YOU'LL ALWAYS REMEMBER

The Editors

Sandra Chastain

Hannah's Hunk

BANTAM BOOKS

NEW YORK · TORONTO · LONDON · SYDNEY · AUCKLAND

HANNAH'S HUNK

A Bantam Book / April 1993

ISBN 0-553-44377-1

Published simultaneously in the United States and Canada

Bantam Books are published by Bantam Books, a division of
Bantam Doubleday Dell Publishing Group, Inc. Its trademark,
consisting of the words "Bantam Books" and the portrayal of
a rooster, is Registered in U.S. Patent and Trademark Office
and in other countries. Marca Registrada. Bantam Books,
666 Fifth Avenue, New York, New York 10103.

PRINTED IN THE UNITED STATES OF AMERICA

OPM   0 9 8 7 6 5 4 3 2 1

One

"I'm absolutely desperate for a *real* man."

Hannah Clendening tapped her pencil against her front teeth and leaned back in her office chair, staring at the April rain splattering against her Long Island cottage window.

"Absolutely desperate!"

"Aren't we all, honey." Daisy, Hannah's motherly assistant, nodded and continued scanning the pages she was reading.

"A tattooed, dirt-breathing, muscle-bound man of the earth."

"Well, I don't know if I'd want to go quite that far."

Hannah came to her feet and strode to the window. "Where is he? In a state the size of New York there must be one man over thirty-five who doesn't shave, doesn't primp, and doesn't look like he's escaped from one of those weird perfume commercials."

"Sure, check any subway or park bench."

But Hannah refused to take Daisy seriously. "I thought the men on Long Island were real people, Daisy. So far the only men I've seen who aren't here for the summer are the mailman—and he's fifty—and Joe, the police captain. Maybe looking for a man who isn't a model is a mistake. If I don't have a hunk by Monday morning, my name will be Hannah C. Mud, with the emphasis on mud."

"I really don't understand your problem. You're the only woman I know who has an all-American male-order wish book and an order blank. Why not just pick one out?"

"Daisy, you're not taking me seriously. They're all too perfect."

Daisy Benson laid down the proposal she was reading and glared at Hannah. "I'm taking you seriously, boss lady. You're desperate for a mature hunk with bad breath and B.O."

Hannah swore. Nobody understood how important it was for Fantasy Romances to succeed. It was her concept, and C. C. Lowen, who owned the company, had given her free rein to hire the most creative writers, artists, and production personnel in the industry.

Fantasy produced two books each month: one from the heroine's point of view, which featured a woman on the cover, and the other from the male point of view, using a man on the cover.

Though Hannah was the editor and personally bought every book, the covers were also her department. Hannah's hunks, the models were called, and Hannah sighed over, fantasized about, and gave her personal approval to each of them.

The January releases had to be special. It was the first anniversary of the line. The heroine had been selected, but this Hannah's hunk had to be awesome. So far Hannah had come up empty.

Razor Cody, the hero in *The Morning After*, was what insiders called a wounded hero. To complicate matters, he was an ex-con and a rebel, and he'd come looking for Miss Rachel Kimbel. Hannah understood Razor, his prickly exterior and his need to thumb his nose at the world. He'd been wronged, and he was out for revenge. The man who portrayed Razor had to be special, very special.

"So, you're looking for an ex-con, why not try the police?" Daisy said vacantly. She'd already turned back to the manuscript she was working on.

Daisy was right. Hannah wondered what she'd been thinking of. She was trying to cast a hero who was an ex-con, what better place to scout for a real man than a prison?

Three days later she was waiting in the parking area of Suffolk County Minimum Security, the country club prison on Long Island.

Under other circumstances she would have been worried, but the man she was to meet was expecting her. Joe, the police captain in Port Jefferson, had made the arrangements. He had given his personal assurance that the man was trustworthy.

Nothing ventured, nothing gained, was the motto Hannah lived by in business, and so far it had gotten her where she wanted to be.

Her personal life was a different story. Nobody knew she'd been a social outcast at two Southern boarding schools where she was supposed to have been turned into a lady. And nobody knew of her brief live-in arrangement with a fellow student at Yale. An even deeper secret was her relationship with her father. She'd been reared by her grandparents and had seen her father only for an occasional lunch or on holidays. Now, because she used her mother's maiden name, nobody knew that C. C. Lowen, corporate director, was in reality Carl Lowenstein, Hannah Clendening's father.

She scanned the parking lot and frowned. She hadn't counted on having television crews and reporters there.

"I'm Wes Varden, *Celebrity* mag," one of the newsmen said as he leaned against her car.

Celebrity magazine. Great! she thought, one of the sleaziest tabloids at the checkout stand.

"Are you here to get a peak at the Don?" he asked.

"The Don?"

"Sure, the junk-bond money-man who's being released today. You're not a reporter?"

"Ah, no. I'm picking up—meeting—someone else. Excuse me, I need to use the air conditioner." She turned on the engine and closed the window, discouraging more questions. Her reason for being there would make great copy but not the kind of publicity Razor's book needed.

The prison doors opened and three men came through. Leaving the engine running, Hannah got out of the car.

A portly man in a silver suit, obviously the Don,

drew all the attention. The second man certainly wasn't her contact; he was nearly sixty. But the third one had definite possibilities.

Even in faded jeans and a chambray shirt, he was impressive. Tall, lanky, muscular, he wore a baseball cap pulled low over his forehead, cowboy boots, and a hands-off attitude that was obvious from ten feet away. With a duffel bag slung over his shoulder, he hung back, allowing the other two men to lead the way.

He was perfect.

Hannah felt a whisper of caution in her stomach flutter to life. No, this wasn't a flutter, this was a full-fledged protest, the ultimate measure of the man's appeal. Hannah smiled and gave a little wave.

Dan Bailey saw her wave and disregarded it. Where the hell was Pete? Being released early was a welcome surprise. Pete's being late to meet him wasn't. Other than the reporters, the only person waiting was a woman. And not just any woman, this one was trouble waiting to happen. The last thing he wanted was to call attention to himself when he was supposed to be on vacation.

Ah, angel. Stop looking at me as if I'm the house special of the day and you're ready to order.

He couldn't imagine who she was there to pick up. Dan turned his head and slid past the reporters. If it had been up to him, he'd have postponed his release a day rather than be recognized as Dan Bailey, the investigative reporter who always got his story, even when it was seldom the one he'd been assigned.

Dan's editor believed that he was in Mexico, relaxing on a sunny beach. Dan had seen the newspaper story about the Don and had thought he was onto something. But he hadn't been sure, and he didn't want to take a chance on his editor getting wind of what he was about to do until he'd proved that his suspicions were right.

"Take it easy for a while, Dan," his editor had warned when he'd completed his last assignment. "You need a rest. Take some time off. You have about six months' vacation coming."

This from the man who'd given Dan an office with a bed and a closet because he stayed in New York too seldom to pay rent on an apartment, Dan thought with a laugh.

But Dan had surprised his boss by agreeing. A vacation was just want he needed, a long one. A few telephone calls later, he'd arranged to become an inmate in the prison where the subject of his investigation was residing. His hunch had been right. Now he just had to get it on paper. For that he needed a place to work—away from his office— until he was ready to break his story.

Dan knew he'd been walking a fine line recently. He even agreed that he needed a vacation, but once he'd read about the Don, he'd known he had to see it through. He'd almost made it past the waiting newsmen, when one reporter called out, "Hey, aren't you—"

Dan recognized that voice and changed his direction, heading toward the woman leaning against the black car. She had the door open and the engine running.

As he strode toward her he watched a breeze catch her hair and sweep it away from her face. He noticed her classic features and wide eyes filled with delight. Because the day was unusually warm for April, she'd removed her jacket, revealing a figure that could never be mistaken for a model's. It was too lush. Those women in the stocking commercials who were all legs didn't have a thing on the blond-haired beauty watching his progress as if she were expecting him.

For a moment they stood staring at each other, the very air around them charged with anticipation. This couldn't be happening, Dan thought. It was like an old movie, replaying itself in his head. A chance meeting of two people who were destined to be together, but only for a short time.

"Even without the trench coat, you're perfect," she said in a low voice, "absolutely—"

Dan had the thought that Sam Spade would have described her voice as whisky-smooth and just as addictive.

"—perfect—even down to the five o'clock shadow." She reached out and caught his arm.

It didn't take Hannah but a moment to understand that the steely look in his eyes meant *whoa*, not thanks for the compliment.

"I'm going to assume you're my guardian angel and you're here to save my neck," he said.

"Don't worry, it's all arranged. I've got a job you're going to be perfect for."

"Hey, Dan!" the insistent reporter called out.

Hannah's hunk put a crooked smile on his lips that didn't match the hardness in his gaze or the tightness of his muscles as he turned his back to the reporter and drew her into his arms. Before she could protest, he lowered his head and captured her lips with his.

Hannah was so shocked that it took her a moment to realize she was being kissed—no, not just being kissed, she was being caressed, groped, fondled, mauled, by a stranger whose touch turned her knees into soggy pasta. She tried to pull away.

"Please?" he whispered in her ear, and this time he allowed a hint of desperation to surface. "Get me away from here fast—and I'll do anything you want."

She was so dazed by what had happened that she answered automatically. "Get in," she whispered, "at least you don't smell bad."

The truth was, he smelled great, and the voice that whispered in her ear was pure melt-in-your-mouth Southern. Yet he looked like a refugee from a rock group. What was going on? She wasn't sure, but Joe had told her that she didn't have to worry. And "worry" was a foreign word to Hannah anyway.

Hannah was absolutely driven, totally efficient, and she simply didn't let things bother her. In her mind this man wasn't a real criminal, he was Razor Cody—or he would be as soon as she got him on the cover of her book.

They drove quickly away, ignoring the reporter running after them. Several minutes passed before he offered an explanation. "I apologize for my behavior. I don't know who you were waiting for back there, but if you'll stop at the first phone, I'll get out."

"Out? You're leaving? Not in this lifetime. You and I have an agreement, and I expect you to live up to it."

Dan couldn't control his surprise. Not surprise at her answer, or because the most beautiful woman he'd seen in a long time was coolly driving away from a prison with a man she didn't even know, but surprised that she seemed determined to keep him.

Nothing that had happened made any sense: his early release, Pete's not being there to pick him up, or Helen of Troy offering him a job.

She didn't look like the kind of woman who got turned on by ex-cons. With her short, sassy haircut, miniskirt, and dark stockings, she might be a stockbroker, or any other career woman. He glanced into the back of her car and saw her attaché case and stacks of typewritten paper. Wait a minute, he thought, maybe he was the one who'd been conned.

"Tell me you're not a reporter, angel."

"I'm not a reporter. I'm creative, but not with words. Tell me you're not an ax murderer."

"There are a few people I've considered strangling, but I'm no good with axes."

She laughed. "Good. Joe said I could trust you."

"Joe? Who's Joe?"

"Joe Dunn," she went on. "He set this up. You do know who I am, don't you?"

"Should I?"

"You—don't—know—Joe?" *Oops!* She'd made an error. Had she come on the wrong day? No, it was the third Saturday in April. Joe had told her three men were to be released, and neither of the other two men could have been her hunk.

"And you aren't Terry Darby, are you?"

"Nope. Terry's in the infirmary with chicken pox."

Hannah sneaked a quick look at her passenger as she eased onto the expressway, and considered her options. He was sprawled out, as much as the small space in her compact car would allow, glaring at her with a dare in his steel gray eyes, a dare that ate up her cool demeanor and left her burning from the heat of his gaze.

"I'm afraid I made a mistake," she said.

Every time she touched the brakes, her skirt slid up an inch. And every inch of long leg she revealed made him conscious that the mistake had been his. He never should have kissed her. He couldn't seem to think about anything except body parts that came in twos—lips, legs, breasts . . .

"Yep," he agreed, "I think you made a mistake, one we both seem to be stuck with at the moment. So, who are you, some kind of nut who gets off on bad guys?"

She hesitated. Maybe it wasn't too late to make it work. After all, he was Razor Cody in the flesh if she'd ever seen him.

"That's pretty much what I am, and a bad guy is exactly what I'm looking for. I'm Hannah Clendening. And if you're not Terry, who are you?"

He still didn't trust her. Something told him that this woman had her own agenda. He was there for her benefit and not the other way around. And Dan Bailey had operated on his hunches for most of his life across most of the world. If she didn't know who he was, he had no intention of telling her. When he found out what she was up to, he'd decide.

"Just call me Rocky, that's a good name for a jailbird."

He might be called maverick, or rogue, or even dude, but Rocky? She gave a secret little smirk. "How about I call you Razor instead?"

"Razor? What the hell? Call me Razor if that makes you happy. Hello, Hannah. Thanks for coming to get me, whoever sent you."

"You might not say that when you find out what I want. Are you hungry?"

"Hungry?" He took another look at the long legs exposed another two inches by the skirt that didn't turn when she did. If she was interested in him for sex, he might as well find out now.

"I'm hungry all right, Hannah, but don't tempt me."

Hannah took a quick look at her potential model. He was hungry for sure, but it wasn't for the hamburger she was about to offer. She'd better take control, or her plan would be shot down before they even got started.

"Now wait a minute, Razor, let's understand each other. I got you away from whoever it was you were trying to avoid back there. But I think he's behind us in the traffic. If you'll cooperate, I can lose him. I don't believe you want to take a chance on making trouble for yourself, do you?"

Dan let out a deep sigh. Trouble? Trouble was the last thing he wanted and just what he'd gotten before he even got out of sight of the prison where he'd spent the longest three months of his life. Any thought he'd had of disappearing into the countryside and finding a place where he could hide until he finished the article was fast becoming an impossibility.

The judge who got him into the jail had done so with Dan's promise that his name be kept out of the press. No publicity. But Wes Varden had been there waiting. He obviously hadn't been on an official assignment, or he wouldn't have been hanging back, Dan thought. But the weasel had seen him and that meant trouble.

Wes had a score to settle with Dan, and he wouldn't hesitate to blow Dan's cover and his story as well. If Wes caught up with them, the woman beside him would be at the mercy of the most sensational tabloid reporter in the country. He realized he had better find a way to protect himself and her too.

Damn! Instead of being halfway back to the city as he'd planned, Dan was in a car with a woman straight out of every sex dream he'd ever had, a brash, confident woman who thought he was an ex-con. She didn't know who he was, but he'd been spotted by somebody who did.

"I said," his guardian angel interrupted his train of thought, "do you want me to lose him?"

"That would be a very good idea, angel, but I warn you this man will stick to you like a bad reputation. And if he catches us, that's what you'll have."

She let out a deep breath and gave a light laugh. "He doesn't know who he's taking on, and don't call me angel."

Hannah waited until the last minute and crossed lanes of traffic, causing car horns to blow and brakes to squeal. She took the next exit, cut through a bank parking lot, and doubled back to catch the expressway entrance that put her behind the car that had been following them.

"Now," she said with satisfaction, "what about some food. A hamburger maybe?"

Dan let out his pent-up breath. If the woman wasn't a reporter, she must be the star of the demolition derby. "Drive, Hannah. We'll talk about food later."

"Whatever you say."

And Hannah hoped he'd say a lot. Rocky wasn't his name but neither was Razor. And she had no idea what kind of crime he'd been serving time for, only that he was exactly what she wanted for the cover of her book.

But there was something disturbing about him. Something she hadn't anticipated. Something dangerous. She pushed away the second thoughts nagging at her.

Hannah headed back to Port Jeff. Taking him to the cottage might not be smart, but at least Daisy would be there. Of course, Hannah could always call Captain Joe, who was practically in walking distance of her house.

"Where are we going?" Razor finally asked.

"I have a cottage overlooking Long Island Sound," she said.

"Fine."

That was the extent of his conversation. Leaning his head back against the seat, he closed his eyes and appeared to sleep until she turned onto Port Jefferson's main street.

Dan sat up and glanced around. He'd been watching Hannah surreptitiously for the last ten minutes. She seemed to know exactly what she was doing. And although he tried, he couldn't see her as one of those women who wrote to men in prison and visited them with some kind of twisted motive. It was obvious she was there for a reason that had nothing to do with him.

She drove expertly, taking the street up the hill to the houses overlooking the Sound, and turned into a small driveway. Now she took a deep breath, shut off the car engine, and put on her best strictly-business demeanor.

"This is where I live. My assistant will be here. We'll go inside and discuss our arrangements. I think that my terms will be satisfactory."

"Your terms?"

"Terms. As in you do something for me, and I pay you for it."

"Now we get down to it." He was beginning to get a bad feeling. She had a job for him, she'd said so. What kind of job would a woman have for a man leaving prison? She had to know that no dangerous criminals were housed where he'd been.

Unless she wasn't as smart as she looked.

Dan would bet his last dime that "dumb blonde" didn't apply to this woman, but then he didn't know her. The possibilities ran through his head. Theft? Blackmail? What was it she'd asked about, ax murders?

Murders? Job? A hit man. If she wanted him to

commit murder, he'd better straighten her out—quick.

"You do understand that my reservations against murder don't apply strictly to axes, Hannah. I'm really not into that kind of crime."

"Neither am I. I think this will be painless enough for you and rewarding too. I'll even provide a place to live until we're finished."

So, it wasn't murder, or if it was, she was being cagey. "About your expectations. You want to clue me in? My agreement isn't a done deed. I think I'll reserve judgment until we've done a bit of negotiating."

"Negotiating?" She had a budget, but it wasn't much. Still, this man was perfect, absolutely perfect, down to the shadow of a beard and the sweaty baseball cap that he'd shoved to the back of his head.

"Yeah, what are you offering and what am I expected to do in return?"

"Let's go inside and I'll try to explain."

She swung her long legs out of the car, planted them on the drive, and started up the steps. Dan claimed his duffel bag and followed, standing on the bottom step where he could enjoy his view of the snug fit of her skirt. He'd been right to worry. She had what it took to be very convincing.

He'd have to explain to her that they were both operating under an alias. His name wasn't Razor, and hers wasn't Hannah. They were Bad Boy and Trouble.

Hannah unlocked the door to the white clapboard cottage and switched on the light. The house was quiet. The only thing moving in the room was the signal on her answering machine. The red light was vibrating like a frustrated bee stuck in a pot of honey.

"We seem to be alone," Dan observed as he closed and locked the door and glanced out the front window. There was no sign of another automobile. If Wes Varden had recognized Dan, he'd be found eventually, but maybe not for a day or two. His plan had been to bunk in with Pete, providing his old friend hadn't rented out the extra bedroom in his apartment. He'd write his story, then tell his editor that his three months' vacation on the beach had been spent in prison.

Hannah was playing her messages.

"Sorry, boss," Daisy's voice said. "Sprained my ankle and couldn't make it to the train. I'll get there, but I'll be a little late. I hope our hunk is the tattooed, dirt-breathing, muscle-bound, gorgeous man of the earth you're looking for."

Then Captain Dunn's voice.

"Sorry about the mix-up, Hannah. Found out that Terry has chicken pox and isn't leaving until the rash is gone. I'll get you another guy. Will this mess up your deadline? I know timing is critical."

"You don't know the half of it, Joe," Hannah said under her breath.

"Tattooed, dirt-breathing, muscle-bound man of the earth? And gorgeous too? That's a lot to live up to," Dan said.

"Don't worry. When I get through, that's what every woman will think about you. By the way, do you have a tattoo?"

Dan Bailey had always considered himself a match for any woman in almost any intimate encounter. He was up for new and innovative ideas. But Hannah Clendening stopped him cold. No, not cold. Cold could never be the operative word, not according to his body. After three months of abstinence, he would have to say that he was more up than usual. In fact he felt like a patriotic American, standing erect and proud.

He gave her a puzzled smile. "Yes, I have a tattoo. This is the first time it's been a job qualification. But what the heck?" He began to unbutton his shirt. "You want to check it out?"

Two

Hannah took a long look at Dan's bare chest. "Razor Cody. You *are* Razor Cody."

"Look, angel, my name is Dan Bailey. I've never even heard of Razor Cody."

"You're Razor Cody in the flesh."

Hannah had thought she was immune to any physical reaction to a man's chest. She'd seen too many of them. But she was wrong. She was wrong about the kind of man she wanted on the cover as well. Tough, yes, but not some muscle-bound hunk. Dan was—sleek, like a panther who was born to stalk his prey.

"Even the sense of danger," she murmured, falling into her habit of thinking out loud. "The air crackles with it. Women react to physical danger. Danger is right. I need to play up the danger."

She called it danger. Dan had called the air charged when he'd stood opposite her at the prison. He'd felt it crackle then, just as she did now, but he'd never had a woman admit it openly before. What was happening?

He frowned. "There may be a physical problem here all right, but danger? You're not into kinky stuff, are you?"

"Bite your tongue. Razor would never do anything kinky. He's out for revenge, yes, determined to punish the person responsible for his losing everything, but he could never hurt Rachel."

"Rachel? Who the hell is Rachel?"

"Why Rachel is—" Hannah shook her head. What was she doing? The man standing in her cottage wasn't Razor Cody. What had he called himself? Dan something or other. She, who remembered every character in her authors' books, couldn't recall this man's last name.

She was losing it. Daisy had warned her that she'd spent so much time creating heroes for the book covers that she wouldn't know a real man if he stood before her stark naked. But even Daisy wouldn't believe this situation.

With a mouth as dry as the Sahara Desert and lungs that sucked in breath as if she were lost in the middle of it, Hannah toyed with the idea of doing the smart thing—pushing him out on the deck and locking the door. He could stay out there until she could get in touch with Joe. That was the smart thing to do. But her mind wasn't thinking smart. She was having trouble forming coherent thoughts of any kind.

All she could see was a chest that might have been the prototype for every Sinbad movie ever made.

Dan what's-his-name had a dynamite chest. It wasn't slick with baby oil or proportioned like a Mr. America candidate. It was lean, powerful, classic, lightly feathered with dark hair spreading from beneath low-slung jeans upward to—

"A spider?" she chortled. "You have a spider tattooed above your—"

"Not just any spider, a tarantula. What's the matter? Does that disqualify me as a dirt-breathing, muscle-bound man of the earth?"

"Not at all. It's perfect."

"And exactly what kind of assignment am I perfect for?"

"It's pretty unique," she said, trying to decide how best to explain what she had in mind. "The shoot has to take place tomorrow. I've already arranged the contract, so I can't wait for Terry to get out of the hospital. You'll have to fulfill it."

"A contract? Wait a minute, lady. I think you ought to know that I'm no hit man."

"That's all right. Joe said that prisoners at the country club aren't real bad guys. The real criminals have to go upstate. Now, how are we going to work this out?"

The situation was getting stickier by the minute. Dan groaned silently. He was wondering the same thing she was: How were they going to work this out?

The woman seemed to think she'd rescued an assassin, and the only time Dan had ever carried a gun had been when he'd tagged along with the rebels in Afghanistan. Surely this Captain Joe didn't know what she had in mind.

Damn! This was getting crazy. All Dan knew was that this had something to do with somebody named Razor. The woman was obsessed with him. That was it. Obsession! And there was a woman named Rachel involved.

This Razor must be something special to make a woman like Hannah kill for him. Without a thought, Dan had voluntarily gotten into the car with a flake.

But Hannah Clendening was an angel. An angel like her wouldn't have to resort to kidnapping to find a man. She looked more like a woman who wanted to solve a murder, not commit one.

Still, she had kidnapped a man—him. The last thing he needed right now was a woman, and, he groaned silently, the thing he needed most right now was a woman.

"Look, Hannah, I don't know what you're planning for me, but I'm not stupid and I'm trying very hard not to behave like this man of the earth you seem to be after. But unless we come to some kind of understanding, one of two things is going to happen."

"What?" she whispered, mesmerized by the tattooed spider. She had the sensation that it was crawling up her backbone. Every shaky breath her ex-con took made it expand and retract. "What is going to happen?"

"I'm either going to get the hell out of here, or—"

"Or?"

"I'm going to put my arms around you, and you're going to learn what it means to be with a man who hasn't had a woman in much too long. I don't think that's a smart move for either one of us."

"You can't go, I need you."

"For what? That's the issue. Is your need personal or business? Personal, I might consider. But if you're trying to hire me for what I think you want, forget it. I don't commit murder."

"I don't want you to commit murder," she said, stunned. "I just want your body, temporarily. Put your shirt back on," she managed to say, and forced her shaky legs to carry her to the kitchen.

"I take it my tattoo passed inspection?"

"Close enough. I'll fix something to eat while I explain."

"I'd be interested in the explanation."

She didn't dare look at him. "I have crab salad. Will that be all right? Or there's a steak in the freezer. I could thaw it."

"Crab salad is fine, but what I'd really like is a beer."

"Sorry, don't drink it. Soda, milk, or iced tea."

"Iced tea."

They were talking, saying the right words, but Hannah was simply staring into the refrigerator, and Dan's gaze was locked onto the short skirt and the back of her legs.

"So who's Razor?" he asked.

"He's my latest hero."

"Your latest?"

"I have to have a new one every month."

The denim fabric of his jeans was turning into rough concrete, pressing like sandpaper against him. For the last ten years he'd covered major news events all over the world. And he'd considered himself as experienced as the next guy. But a woman who picked up men being released from prison at the rate of one a month was a first.

"You mean like ice cream?" he asked curiously.

She took a plastic dish from the refrigerator, backed out, and turned around. "Ice cream?"

Planting her gaze on his face instead of his chest was no help. His skin was deeply bronzed. This was a man who was no stranger to the sun. Little lines radiated out from the corners of his eyes, giving him the appearance of laughing even when his lips were narrowed in annoyance. While she'd fumbled in the refrigerator, he'd removed his baseball cap, revealing intense smoky-gray eyes that blurred her concentration and left her standing in the middle of the kitchen holding her crab salad like a talisman. Thick locks of dark hair reached his shoulders and curled around the collar of his shirt. As he talked his movements allowed a flash of silver to show through the strands of his hair—an earring. Razor Cody with an earring? Why not?

"Yeah, ice cream, like flavor of the month."

"Something like that," she managed to say. "Of course, each of my heroes is different. They all have their own distinct personalities and appearances. But the most important thing is that on command, they come alive for me."

"I'm afraid to ask, but what's the command?"

"That's just an expression. It simply means that he literally has to jump on the cover when I see him."

That did it. Dan took hold of the counter and held on. He'd stepped into some erotic fantasy, and he'd become as turned on as its creator was. He'd never auditioned for a job in bed before. Well . . . maybe once. He'd been sixteen and had wanted to progress beyond grass cutting for the wealthy widow who'd hired him. As it turned out, he'd split his duties that summer between the yard and the house. But that was a long time ago.

In the last few years he'd stopped auditioning. He'd given up on any long-term relationship at all. The kind of life he led didn't leave much room for a woman, even if he'd found one he was interested in.

Until now. Hell, now he was so hot that he could have thawed out that steak simply by touching it. Temporary use of his body sounded just fine. "Where's your bed?"

That question jerked Hannah back to reality. "Bed?"

"I'm not looking for a job. I still have one, at least I think I do. But I might consider your offer, in exchange for a place to stay for a few days. You like my body, and yours is spectacular. So let's do it."

"Do it? Mr. Bailey, my offer does not include the use of my bed!"

So what if she was a fruitcake? A woman with a body like Hannah's could get away with a lot. He'd go along. He could be calm and patient. "All right, where do you keep *your* covers?"

"Covers?" She played the conversation back in her mind and began to laugh.

"I've had some odd conversations, Hannah, but this has to be the weirdest. Just tell me straight out, what do you want me to do, and where do you want me to do it?"

"Oh, I don't want you, I mean, not you personally. I just want your body. I'm looking for a model for the cover of my next Fantasy Romance."

"A model? You want me to be a model?"

"Yes. It would only take a few hours, and it could make you famous."

Famous Investigative Reporter Becomes Romance Pin-up Model. That was just what he needed, to be plastered all over the cover of a sex magazine, when he was trying to keep a low profile. Dan pulled out a stool from beneath the counter and sat. That thought had taken the starch out of his denim.

"Start at the beginning, angel—sorry, Hannah. You came to the prison to pick up a guy who was going to be a model for a magazine cover?"

"Book cover." Belatedly, Hannah set the container of salad on the counter and took plates from the cabinet. She added a head of lettuce and box of crackers as she talked.

"I'm Hannah Clendening, editor-in-chief for Fantasy Romance Novels. I'm looking for a man to illustrate our January cover. Razor Cody, the book hero, has just been declared innocent of the crime for which he'd been imprisoned. He's out for revenge. And the object of that revenge is Miss Rachel Kimbel. It's Razor I'm looking for."

"A tattooed, dirt-breathing, muscle-bound man of the earth. I know."

"That's right."

"You left out gorgeous."

"That was Daisy's addition."

"And Daisy is?"

"My editorial assistant. And Dan is?"

"Dan Bailey is an aroused idiot who is also a news correspondent."

"Dan Bailey—Oh!"

"I thought you might remember. Dan Bailey, the reporter who broke the story of the head of one of our national agencies taking a million-dollar bribe from an arms dealer in Hong Kong."

"That's right. You're the man who takes all the risks. You must lead an exciting life."

Dan could have told her that it hadn't been exciting for a long time. For every wrong he exposed, there were hundreds that never would be uncovered. And sometimes the wrong people were hurt by his stories. There were so many things he wished he could do over. Maybe the story he was working on now would be a start.

"I'm sorry. I didn't recognize you." Hannah knew him by reputation. Everybody in publishing did. The bad boy of the publishing field, the man who cultivated the power brokers and the jet-setters and enjoyed the lifestyle they provided.

"I don't suppose you want to tell me what you were doing in jail?"

"You're right. I wouldn't."

"Now I understand why you were so anxious to get away. One of those reporters recognized you."

"You got it, angel. Now his curiosity is aroused, and you're—involved."

Hannah gulped. At least he didn't say she was aroused, although he wouldn't be far wrong. Daisy was right, a real man affected her a lot differently than one of her book heroes.

Hannah filled their glasses with ice and placed a pitcher of iced tea on the counter. "You were actually a prisoner there, weren't you?"

"I don't think you need to know any more than you already do."

"How did you plan to get back to town? Walk?"

"No, Pete, my friend, was supposed to be there when they released me tomorrow, then they let me out today instead. I left a message on his machine, but apparently he didn't get it. May I use your phone?"

"Sure, it's on my desk." She made a gesture to the corner where he'd find a desk, if he managed to get under the stacks of manuscripts that occupied all the space not taken up by her computer. She watched him move across the room and let out a sigh of regret. He wasn't an ax murderer, but she wasn't certain that he'd consent to becoming a cover model either.

For a moment she was sorry that she'd corrected his impression that she wanted his body. Hannah had always gone with her instincts, and her instinct now was that she might have missed one of the great opportunities of her life: a personal audition by Dan Bailey, the hottest lover since Lady Chatterley's lodge-keeper.

She took two plates and placed them on a tray. Next she added lettuce to the plates, scooped a dollop of salad, and dropped it on top, openly listening all the while.

"Pete, where the hell were you?"

Her unexpected guest was holding the phone beneath his chin while he buttoned his shirt. With no thought of being watched, he unzipped his jeans and tucked his shirttail back inside his pants, stretching to smooth out the bunched-up fabric. Hannah gulped. There it was again, the feel of fuzzy tarantula feet shimmying across her skin.

"And you didn't get the word that I was being released early? No, I don't need you to come for me. Someone else picked me up." He was absently studying her computer, turning it on as he talked. "No, Wes Varden was there. No, I don't think so, but I'm afraid he spotted me. I think I'll hide out for a few days. Cover me, will you?"

Hannah added two napkins to the tray, picked up the crackers, and started toward the sliding glass doors leading to the deck. "The food's ready, Dan. Bring the tea, and we'll eat out here."

Dan nodded and kept talking. "As a matter of fact, yes. I am with a woman."

Hannah didn't hear the rest of the conversation. She'd already eavesdropped shamelessly, and suddenly she didn't want to hear any more.

Moments later Dan followed her outside, his expression reflecting his appreciation of the view of the harbor. The shoreline was crescent shaped, housing the dock for the ferry, the inn, and a number of businesses, some of which dated back to her grandfather's time, when the residents had been fishermen and boat builders.

The scene was picture-postcard beautiful—the blue water, sailboats of every description, yachts, and a goregeous sky.

A brisk spring breeze topped the waves with frothy whitecaps that curled toward the house, winked, and slapped the rock wall that held up the dock.

"This is quite a place, angel."

"Look, Mr. Bailey—"

"Dan. I think we're past being formal, don't you?"

"Look, Dan, let's get one thing clear. I'm not an angel, not yours or anyone else's."

"Good. I like my women naughty."

"I'm not your woman." She wasn't naughty either, but she couldn't say she wasn't tempted.

"Fair's fair. If I'm your man, you're my woman."

"If you do become my hero for January, I expect you to call me Ms. Clendening."

"I don't think I could work in that kind of atmosphere."

"Well, maybe you could call me Hannah."

"All right, I'll call you Hannah for now. Tell me about this flavor-of-the-month process. Where do you find your other heroes? And how many are there?"

"Sit down, Dan. You'll be the twelfth one. The others came from agencies, friends, from the street. One was a professional baseball player."

"Do you pick them by profession, or strictly by looks?"

Maybe this wasn't a bad idea. Dan was always looking for stories that were different. He might cover a crime one month, a political issue the next, and something as heartwarming as the adoption of the Romanian children the next.

As he picked up his fork to eat, Dan Bailey sketched out the lead for a proposed article on beautiful women who pick and choose their men on a monthly basis. Not Black Widows who prey on the unsuspecting male, but golden Valkyries. The research for this kind of article was right up his alley. And Hannah Clendening was the perfect target. That thought blew his mind.

"The selection process varies, depending on the book."

Hannah waited until he started to eat, then rose and headed toward the kitchen. "Excuse me a moment, please. I'd better call Daisy, or she'll hail a taxi and come up here. Our budget doesn't allow for that."

Dan watched her as she punched in the numbers on the phone. She spoke, then held on for what seemed like too long, then spoke again. As she hung up she glanced through the glass doors and caught sight of him watching. The guilty look that flashed across her face told him that it hadn't been Daisy she'd been speaking with.

As she walked back to the table, Dan could tell that she was mentally arguing with herself.

"Did he vouch for me?"

"Who?"

"The police captain. Wasn't that who you called?"

"Yes. Captain Joe's checking with the judge who sentenced you."

Dan chewed his food thoughtfully, trying to find somewhere to plant his gaze other than on her legs. He tried her hair. No help, it was a taffy-colored silk fan that seemed to accent her words with its movement. Her eyes weren't the answer either. They were blue, so blue that she could have modeled color contact lenses.

He searched for a flaw in the woman sitting across from him, searched and finally found it. She had long, slender fingers, capped by beautiful, fiery red fingernails. All except one. The thumbnail on her right hand was covered with a bandage.

A flaw, a vulnerability! He wanted to shout, then tempered his reaction with the picture of that finger between her lips, full, luscious lips that begged to be kissed until they were swollen and red.

As if she were responding to his mental picture, she thrust the side of her thumb in her mouth and nibbled absently at the skin at the corner of her nail.

"So? Where does that leave us?" he asked, his tone making it clear that he was asking about the job, but that wasn't what he really wanted to know.

"Look, Dan, let me lay my cards on the table."

"I'm listening."

She lifted her glass of iced tea and took a long, slow swallow. "I thought I had the man for the book cover selected. I already explained that I can't wait for Terry. I simply have to assume you're not a bad guy. The shoot is scheduled for tomorrow because it's the only free day my photographer has. You have to be my model."

Dan had no intention of being anybody's model. His professional reputation would be in shreds when his associates got wind of the fact that he was posing for romance novel covers. But he couldn't resist the desperation in her voice as she described her situation. Maybe he could think of another answer.

"What exactly does a book cover model do?"

"This was the agreement I had with Terry. You'll be photographed in several poses, alone. Then we'll bring in a female model and repeat the process for the clinch shot. Once we have all the test photographs, I'll select the ones we'll use for sketches."

"The clinch?"

"Yes, the embrace between the hero and heroine. The writers hate them, but the book buyers don't. We've tried to make our presentation a bit different. The front cover features just the hero, with the clinch on the back."

"And then what?"

"You'll stay here until I'm certain that the negatives are developed and we have good choices. Then you're free to go. The artist will paint the picture from the photograph."

"And will the painting look like me?"

"I certainly hope so."

"Then I'll have to say no."

"Why? I know all this sounds strange. I promise, it won't be hard."

Dan could have argued. From the moment he'd laid eyes on Hannah Clendening, his body had felt as if it were encased in heated mud, the temperature shifting from extra warm to boiling.

Breathe fast, he told himself. Animals pant when they're overheated to cool themselves. Hell, he was practically panting now, and that just made the temperature climb.

"It isn't the posing that's the problem. I could probably get through that, all things being equal, but I don't want my picture spread all over the book racks. I have to protect my image as a professional. I don't want the world to think I'm investigating romance."

"And you think being on my book cover could harm your image? I don't think so. At least my stories are uplifting, one-on-one stories of commitment."

" 'Uplifting' is the key word here. I've been in jail for three months. I don't think this would be a smart move, angel."

Hannah tried not to laugh. She fought the mirth that curled the corners of her mouth, but she simply couldn't control the direction her mind took following that statement.

"Dan Bailey undercover? Uplifting assignment? Well, yes, undercover experience is good," she managed to quip, "and uplifting too, particularly for this job."

"Hannah!" he began. Then he began to laugh. And that surprised even him. Light and agreeable on occasion, a dry cynical chortle and an occasional scornful chuckle pretty much made up his laugh quotient. But a real laugh that started with a little rumble and grew in proportion to the picture it was responding to, was rare.

"That wasn't what I meant," he finally said.

"I know. It was awful of me to laugh. But the truth is, I'm desperate. Isn't there something I can offer you to make you change your mind? The money isn't a lot, but it's pretty good for the time you'll spend. And it isn't the first time you've been on the cover of a book."

"It isn't the money. It's the exposure and the time. I really do have a deadline too. And I have to find a place to settle in and write this article while it's still hot on my mind and I can still get to my sources."

"You need a place to write? Fine, you have one. There's my computer. I have a printer, a modem, and a fax machine. What else to you need?"

"Silence and no distractions. And, Hannah, there's no way in hell that you and I could work in the same house and not be a distraction to each other."

"Dan, it really is unlikely that the world will know that the model on this book cover is Dan Bailey, unless you tell them. Your name won't be on the book. Our authors always send in photos of famous people to be used on their covers. You won't believe how many times we've done John F. Kennedy, Jr. What about it?"

Dan finished the last of his salad and laid his fork and knife in the middle of the plate. He glanced at his watch and rose from the table. "I don't know. Maybe. You have a television?"

"Yes, in the bedroom. Upstairs. Why?"

"Bedroom?" That figured. The more he tried to plant his attention on business, the more it became clear that he was going to have to leave Port Jefferson to do so.

"Yes. I usually don't get home until late. I don't get a chance to watch much television until I'm in bed. I'll show you."

"That's all right. I'll find it."

He left her clearing the table, watching him climb the stairs as she worked.

The room with the television set had a large oak bed with a heavy headboard and footboard. There were sliding glass doors which opened out onto a balcony. Planted before the doors was an antique brass telescope mounted on a captain's wheel. The room was masculine, clean, and almost austere in it's simplicity.

There were no chairs, except one window seat that wasn't convenient to the television set. He sat on the bed, picked up the remote control unit, and turned the channel to one of the city's most professional news programs.

He watched for a few minutes before they ran the film he was looking for—the Don, leaving the prison accompanied by his underlings and his attorneys. And there he was, walking away from the camera.

Just as Wes Varden called out to him, the film ended and the camera focused on the newscaster again.

"Damn!" Of all the people to meet outside the prison, he had to run into Wes. And he knew Wes was too good a reporter to forget what he'd seen. *Celebrity* magazine was after scandal, and Dan leaving the prison could be a bigger story than the Don, especially since there was a beautiful blonde involved. Wes printed smut, and he could manufacture it when there was none. By tomorrow Wes would know who Hannah was and where she lived.

Dan walked to the window. On either side were bookcases filled with colorful novels. Fantasy Romances. She was right about the men on the covers. They were different, interesting and very masculine without being refugees from Malibu Beach. And the women were just as stunning.

He could see Hannah standing on the deck below, the ocean breeze tousling her hair and pressing the silk blouse against her full breasts. Switching off the television, he made his way back downstairs, then stood in the doorway and watched her for a long time. He knew this was the last place he ought to be. Even if she stayed upstairs and he worked at the desk, she would be a distraction. Hell, she'd be a distraction now even if he moved into the city.

"Did you find out what you wanted to know?" Hannah asked.

"Maybe. Where is your car registered?"

"Why?"

"Wes Varden is a reporter for the worst of the tabloids. If he's on my trail, I have to make plans."

"Why would Wes Varden be on your trail?"

"Because he would like nothing better than to discredit me and steal my story. He was with *World Today* magazine once. He lost out on a job he expected to get, and he believes I was responsible."

"The car is leased by my company," Hannah answered, drawing Dan back to the present. "It has a city license plate, and my name isn't on it."

"Well, that will hold him up, but it won't stop him."

"Why will it matter?" she asked curiously. "Once you write your article, everybody will know."

"Yes," he said, "but in the meantime Wes isn't above coming up with some sensational story about you and me."

Three

Hannah saw the police car arrive and met the captain at the front door. "Come in, Joe. You know you really didn't have to come up here."

"I know. This isn't official, but I couldn't go off duty without touching base. You okay, Hannah?" Joe ambled around the room, touching the back of the couch, the edge of the desk, as if he might be considering making her an offer for the lot.

"I'm fine. I just have to convince Mr. Bailey that he won't damage his reputation by being a book-cover model."

Joe frowned. "I don't think this will damage his reputation, but I'm not sure about yours. The judge vouches for him, though I'm not sure I trust him. Where is he, anyway?"

"Here," Dan answered, stepping into the open doorway from the deck. "You can relax, chief. My reputation is a bad rap. But I guess you've heard that before, haven't you?"

"Relax, son. What's got you wound up so tight?"

Dan knew that by now Joe Dunn would have satisfied himself that he was who he said he was. Dan couldn't blame Joe for being concerned about Hannah. She was the kind of woman who attracted men and trouble without trying.

"I spent three months in prison, Captain. Guilty or not, it tends to make a man a bit suspicious."

"That's what happens when you work with the criminal element. But don't worry. You're in good hands here. I just wanted to make sure you didn't misunderstand Hannah's plan."

Dan gave a dry laugh. "Misunderstand? I'm picked up by a cover girl who lusts after my body and believes I'm somebody called Razor. Then she tells me she's put out a contract that I have to honor. How could I possibly misunderstand?"

Hannah sympathized with Dan. But she didn't dare give in to her inclination to laugh. It was time she acted like an editor. The first thing she needed to do was apologize.

"I'm really sorry, Dan. I can see why you might be confused by what happened. I do tend to make my heroes human, but Razor really is a fictional outlaw. You're the real thing. I promise it's only your body I want to use, and I'll keep your identity secret."

Dan lifted his eyebrows and gave the police captain a mock-baffled look. "What can I say, Captain, I rest my case."

That was the moment Daisy arrived, opening the door and limping in as if she expected a riot in progress and she was the one to end it.

"What are you doing here, Daisy?" Hannah asked. "You should have stayed home and rested your ankle."

"And miss meeting Razor Cody in the flesh? Not in this lifetime. Where is he?" Daisy asked, plodding past Joe and coming to a sudden stop in front of Dan Bailey. She nodded appreciatively. "I'll have to hand it to you, Hannah, you've outdone yourself this time. He's perfect. What are you going to do about Rachel?"

"I thought I'd put a blond wig on the model for Stacy, the heroine in last month's book."

"Not good, Hannah. She's too short. Dan here is Heathcliff on the moor, dark, brooding. You need to set him against a tall, willowy blonde. Light and Dark. Passion and Innocence. Fire and Ice."

Joe matched Dan's baffled expression with one of his own.

"It's too late for that, Daisy. She's already been hired. This is the weekend, remember. The shoot is set for tomorrow."

Daisy continued to study Dan.

"Something wrong?" he finally drawled.

"Not a thing, honey. I can't see one single thing I'd change, except maybe your age. No, check that. If I were picking and choosing, I'd leave yours alone and change mine. How do you feel about older women?"

"Depends on the woman. I can be had."

"Yep, sense of humor too. What about the tattoo?"

Dan started unfastening his shirt. "You want to see it too?"

"No, that's okay." Daisy climbed onto one of the bar stools and rested her ankle on the one next to it. "Hannah, he's definitely Razor. Stacy's too short. I think you need a heroine with height. Stand over here by him."

"Daisy, don't be silly."

"I'm not. I think you'll see what I'm thinking."

Daisy pulled herself up and, balancing on one leg, turned Dan toward the mirror over the mantel. She motioned Hannah over beside him.

"Daisy, sit down!" Hannah said in exasperation.

"Get over here and I will."

Hannah gave a palms-up gesture of resignation and stepped over to the mirror. Daisy was as stubborn as she was loyal. The rest of the staff tolerated her affectionately.

"No," Daisy directed, "stand in front. Dan, loop your arms around her waist."

Dan gave a resigned shake of his head and followed Daisy's directions.

"This isn't necessary, Daisy," Hannah protested, stepping in front. She was used to Daisy, but she knew others found her a bit trying. Hannah tilted her head back to apologize to Dan for her assistant's bossy behavior.

Dan's arms closed around Hannah at the same moment their gazes met. Hannah might have retained her equilibrium if they hadn't touched. The room seemed to turn, the light swirling around them like a carousel awash with movement and flashing colors. Hannah's lips parted. Her pulse took a shuffle-step as she tried to speak. There was something she needed to say, but the words got caught up in the changing patterns.

Dan wasn't doing any better. He had gone along with the woman's fantasy. He owed her something. She'd been kind enough to get him away from the prison and offer him the use of her computer while he wrote his story. And she was the most stunning woman he'd been with in a long time, but this instant flare of heat at their touch was something he hadn't counted on. His defenses were at an all-time low, his body already primed to a response level that threatened to explode. Now he was holding her and it was as if they were the only two people in the room.

"Whoopee! I knew it," Daisy chortled with elation. "Better step back, Joe, we're in immediate danger of meltdown."

"Looks like it," Joe agreed, his attention planted on Daisy rather than Hannah.

Daisy was clapping her hands. "It's hot. Basil St. John, the mystery man, without the mask, and Brenda with stars in her eyes."

Joe shook his head in disbelief. "You're dating yourself, Daisy. Only us old folks know about Brenda Starr and her mystery man. I don't even think that movie they made got out of Brooklyn." .

"Don't knock Brooklyn, Captain. I'm from Brooklyn, and we know a good thing when we find it."

It was Daisy's mention of stars in her eyes that broke the spell for Hannah. She swallowed and pulled her attention back to the mirror. Daisy was right about the comparison. Dan Bailey was more intriguing than any mystery man. And there were stars in her eyes.

"You're right," she said, her voice fluttering lightly. "The Stacy model won't do. I'll get on the phone and find a tall blonde."

Dan, still caught up in the moment, tightened his grip. His words surprised even him. "We already have one—you."

"Me? I'm not a model."

"And I am?"

"But you—I—I mean this is different. What would my staff think? I have to work with these people."

She looked panic-stricken. What the hell? Dan thought, he'd done a lot worse to get a story in the past. She'd promised that no one would learn his name, and he owed her something for coming to his rescue. Besides, there was something about those starry blue eyes staring at him in the mirror that intrigued him.

"The only way I'll do this thing, Hannah, is if you do it with me. I'll do your book cover, and then I'll stay here and write my story. That's my deal. Take it or leave it."

Pete would raise the roof and accuse him of making a totally irrational decision based purely on old-fashioned lust. Even as he was agreeing, Dan could hear a little voice warning him that he'd better get out of Hannah's life while he still could.

If Wes found them, they were sunk.

Resignation played across his face, resignation and concern. Hannah could see and read it, for it matched her own expression. The man was a rake, a maverick, or he wouldn't have agreed. She was being equally reckless, for she knew that she wouldn't refuse. If eyes were the windows of the soul, she was lost, because hers were sending signals of their own at the same time she was nodding.

Daisy might be mother-wise and foolishly outspoken, but she'd been wrong about one thing. Hannah wasn't too caught up in her imaginary heroes to know a real live man when she met one.

And Dan knew that she did.

He was nodding too.

Joe left after a whispered conversation about wisdom with Hannah, and a warning to Dan that he'd be watching. Hannah agreed to be careful. She put Daisy in her old childhood room, designated the master bedroom for Dan, and claimed the couch for herself.

"No way," Dan disagreed. "I'll take the couch."

"And your feet will hang over the end," she argued. "I shanghaied you, and the least I can do is offer you a comfortable bed. After all, I don't suppose those mattresses in prison are worth much."

"I've slept on worse."

They were standing in the upstairs hall, only inches apart.

Hannah started to move around Dan. At the same time, Dan moved away. They touched, jerked away, and averted their eyes. But the damage was done. Desire flared between them like a force field.

"I want you to be comfortable," she said softly. "Tension lines show in the face."

"Listen, Hannah, the only way I'm going to get rid of the tension is for the two of us to share that bed, and I don't think that's going to happen with a chaperone."

"No, I don't think so. I mean . . . this is a business arrangement, nothing more. I hardly know anything about you. A personal relationship wouldn't be smart."

"You got that right," Daisy's voice interrupted. "I think we want the 'before' look on Razor's cover, not the 'after.' I'm ready for some dinner. How about you?"

Dinner was the last thing Dan was ready for, but at least it was a physical act on which he could focus. He turned and started down the stairs, still caught up in the thought of the "after" Daisy had mentioned.

Daisy followed Dan, and before he knew it he was grating cheese for a pizza while she sat on a stool and made the crust, chattering all the time about Hannah.

"Hannah's the heart of the company. Came up with the Fantasy Romance concept and hired the entire crew."

"I'm surprised that two paperbacks a month is a big enough venture to interest a publisher."

"Wouldn't be, except that in addition to the literary publishing company of which we're an offshoot, a couple of newspapers, and a television station, the owner is literally rolling in old money. He didn't expect us to break even for two years. We're close and it's because of Hannah."

"No, it's because of C.C.," Hannah said as she claimed a stool at the counter and watched her associate knead and roll out the dough. "He's willing to settle for reasonable profits instead of making the bottom line the final control. I don't approve of his lifestyle, but professionally I respect him."

Dan felt an unexpected twinge of envy at Hannah's relationship with her publisher. He couldn't begin to imagine having a relationship with a workaholic like Hannah. He'd seen enough of career women in the past. He had nothing against them. At least he didn't think he was a chauvinist. But he was too opinionated, too strong, to deal with that kind of woman in his personal life. He liked his women soft. Well, maybe he was a bit chauvinistic. He renewed his grating with vigor, shoving the last tiny piece of cheese down against the grater.

"Damn!"

"What's wrong?" Hannah hurried over to him, caught sight of the skinned knuckle, and stopped short.

"I grated my—finger," Dan said slowly, his gaze planted forcefully on Hannah.

"Don't touch him!" Daisy snapped. "I don't want that cheese melted until it's in the oven. Get a bandage, Hannah." Daisy motioned her toward the steps and turned back to examine Dan's finger.

"It's nothing," Dan protested, wrapping his finger

in a paper napkin and moving out of the suddenly warm kitchen and onto the deck.

"You're right," Daisy raised her voice, talking to the empty air as she returned her attention to her crust. "Suck on it. That always makes it feel better. At least that's what Hannah says."

Dan's throat tightened. His tongue tingled. He had visions of tasting something else, something pleasant and feminine. He was still holding the paper napkin against his finger. He'd never sucked his thumb as a child. But he'd seen Hannah's thumb. He'd seen her worry it with her lips. Maybe he—"Damn!" He was the one going kinky.

Daisy's pizza was good. At least Hannah assumed it was. After she finished her slice, she couldn't remember what kind of topping was on it.

Daisy was still talking. Dan had turned silent, watching Hannah with an intensity that grew rather than lessened.

"How long have you been in publishing?" he finally asked Hannah.

"Six years. You?"

"Ten, if you count the time I spent as a copyboy when I was in college. How'd you get started?"

"Degree in literature and fine arts from Yale one day and straight on to New York City the next. Used all the money I inherited from my grandfather to support myself the first two years, until I finally found a job as an editorial assistant for a romance publishing house."

"Until they folded," Daisy inserted. "They were one of the casualties of the kind of conglomerates who've bought out almost every small publishing company. Great books, but the parent company shut them down."

"Yes, they did," Hannah admitted, "three months after I was finally made a full editor."

"Sounds like me. My first job was to cover city hall for the *Atlanta Times*. When it folded, I moved over to Associated Press."

"At least you didn't close that down too. After my first job I was hired by a competing house. It eventually folded too. I was beginning to feel like a jinx. You know what you want, but you can't find anyone who believes in you enough to take a chance."

Anyone who believes in you! Dan knew what that meant. The minute he'd started his journalism career, his father had slammed the door that was already half closed. The Baileys were lawyers, judges, politicians—and their worst enemies were reporters. By joining the opposition, Dan had jumped ship, and his ship had sailed away as fast as it could move. He'd stayed in touch with his mother for a while, but his calls seemed to start new confrontations and thus had become less frequent through the last years.

"So how'd you tie up with Fantasy?" he asked.

"I—I've known C. C. Lowen all my life. When the second company closed down, he took a chance on me, let me add a paperback romance line to his literary empire."

"You say he owns a newspaper? I don't recognize the name."

"He's the silent partner. Some people call him cold. Some say he's the rare man who is willing to give others the credit for everything his company does. In any case, he manages to stay out of the spotlight," Hannah explained.

Unless he's with you, Dan thought. C.C. might try to keep a low profile, but there was no way in hell anybody would ever be ignored if Hannah were hanging on to his arm.

"So what else does C.C. do, besides let you spend his money on auditioning men?"

"He gets married."

That stopped Dan. There was no obvious connection between Hannah's statement and Dan's question.

"What does that mean?"

Daisy let out a sound of disbelief. "Our illustrious leader has just married for the fifth time. And he hasn't considered me yet. I think it's his hobby."

"Expensive hobby," Dan commented.

"That's C.C." Hannah said in an odd, low voice.

Daisy took a resigned look at the table and shifted her weight on her sore ankle. "I'm going to leave these dishes with you. I've got to get off my ankle. I'll take the couch. That way I won't have to climb the stairs."

"But, Daisy—" Hannah began.

"I've got editing to do," Daisy went on. "Can I trust you to behave yourselves?"

"Of course," Hannah said.

"Probably not," Dan said at the same time. "But you don't have to sleep down here. I'll help you upstairs."

He scooped Daisy up into his arms and carried her up to the bedroom, depositing her on the frilly bed in the smaller room. He glanced around. "A teenager's room?"

"Yep. Hannah's. She lived here after her mother died. Her father remarried, but he never quite got around to sending for her. She was too close in age to his new wife. After her grandmother and then her grandfather died, she was sent away to boarding school in Virginia."

"It looks a bit—"

"Bare? You're right. Hannah always travels light. Never gets attached to anything. Her philosophy is, if you don't become attached to things, you won't be hurt if you lose them. She's still that way. Has the worst-looking desk in the smallest office on the floor. Nobody else wanted it."

"But her grandfather loved her, apparently."

"Apparently. But he was pretty old and didn't know much about little girls. Then, too, he was gone a lot. Left Hannah with a housekeeper. That's when she turned to books. She was lonely, and the people she read about became more real than the ones she knew. So far as I know, I'm the closest thing to a real friend she has. And she wouldn't have me if I didn't force the relationship."

"What about the father?"

"He tries. But the jury is still out on that relationship."

Dan felt a sinking sensation in the pit of his stomach. He knew about parents who abandoned their child. His mother hadn't died, she'd simply become the wife of a judge and the mother of a senator, Dan's brother Robert. There'd been no official housekeeper for Dan, only Mattie the cook. She'd done the best she could for the youngest son of an ambitious family who expected more than he could give.

"Shall I bring up your bag, Daisy?"

"Thanks, but Joe already did. Now, there's a real man for you. Did you know him before you became a convict?"

"Sorry, no. You interested?"

"Honey, I'm always interested. I like my men living and breathing—breathing heavy, if possible. I leave the fantasies to Hannah."

Dan paused in the doorway. "Is that what I am to Hannah?"

"I hope not. And I want you to know that after tomorrow, I'm out of here—at least for a couple of days. Got to give my ankle a few days to heal before I start checking out Joe."

"You're serious, aren't you?"

"That I am. Always call them like I see them."

"And what do you see for Hannah and me?"

"Well, I'm having a problem there. I can't seem to get through the fog on my glasses. I'd say that if you don't burn each other up, this will turn into a very interesting session."

"Session?"

"Yep. Good thing that Razor is a sensual man. I wouldn't want the readers to be misled. Night, Dan. Remember, great athletes abstain the night before a big event."

"I've heard that." He grinned. "I could never figure out why."

"Simple. The hungrier you are for the prize, the sweeter the victory. Sweet dreams, Razor. Don't worry about tomorrow. Keep a stiff—well, maybe not. Tension isn't the only thing that shows in a photo shoot."

Four

Dan slept on the pull-out couch. His feet did hang over and his back got a cramp, but it wasn't the lumpy mattress that kept him awake, it was the thought of the soft one upstairs.

And the woman sleeping on it.

Finally Dan gave up and went outside to sit on the deck, where he watched the lights of passing ships. He hadn't had much free time in the last few years. He'd always been on his way to someplace or on his way back. Unpack one suitcase and pack another.

He was tired. He hadn't known how tired until now. Daisy and Hannah had retired for the night, leaving him to face spending the evening at the computer or watching the stars. The stars won, the stars and thoughts of the woman who'd cast him as a wounded hero.

Wounded hero. The wounded part fit; he wasn't certain about the hero part. He'd been wound-ed, both physically and emotionally. A piece of shrapnel he'd picked up in Lebanon still gave his knee a twinge when it rained. And for every new assignment, it seemed to take him longer to build up his enthusiasm. He'd been given credit for making the world a little better. He wasn't certain that qualified him as a hero. But tonight he was having some serious thoughts about where he was going next.

In spite of the trouble he'd been involved in and the reputation he had as a ladies' man who wasn't above using his connections—both high-level and low-life—to get the story, he knew he was a good reporter. The bottom line was, he wasn't having fun anymore. And in the end, he doubted that he'd really changed the world in any way.

Even so, he wasn't ready to hang it up and take a job behind a desk. Ideas were a dime a dozen. It was chasing down the elusive lead, finding the hidden information, discovering the truth, that once gave him the ultimate high.

He looked out over the water and thought of his horrified reaction to Hannah's request. As it turned out, he'd enjoyed their double-edged quips this evening. Even Daisy's presence hadn't slowed down their perfect rapport. Tonight had been fun. And fun had been in short supply in his life for the last few years. The photo shoot the following day might be another story.

Dan Bailey, a model. That ought to thrill his straitlaced old Southern family. Still, he'd done worse in his life, including the night he'd gotten his tattoo. Being a cover model couldn't be any harder than pretending to be a biker when he didn't even know how to ride a motorcycle. He hoped what he had to do for this job wasn't as big a surprise as the gang initiation—a ride through hell and a tarantula on his chest. He'd gotten the story and a conversation piece that had remained long after he'd sold the article and the bike.

Hannah had told him that his name wouldn't be on the book cover anywhere. She'd told him she needed him and had made him laugh. Maybe it was the laugh that had done it, for somehow he'd agreed.

Standing in her upstairs window overlooking the deck, Hannah watched Dan. She couldn't tell whether he was studying the harbor or lost in his thoughts. She wished she could be that calm, but she was keyed up instead. For a woman who'd always kept herself totally focused on her work, she was suddenly fragmented.

Razor Cody, the hero who had captured her full attention for the last weeks, quite simply paled in comparison to Dan Bailey. She didn't have an explanation for her sudden obsession with a real man. But it was happening, and she seemed powerless to stop it.

Hannah paced back and forth from the bed to the window, picking up a proposal from one of her favorite authors and putting it down again without turning on the light, much less glancing at it.

She couldn't understand her preoccupation with Dan Bailey. He was like her father, the kind of powerful man she avoided, always on the move, convinced that he was always right. She wondered how he'd convinced the inmates he was one of them, then recalled the way he'd looked and talked when she first picked him up. The same qualities she'd looked for in her model made him successful in his job. She was glad there was no law against sexual magnetism.

Tomorrow loomed before her. By now he was probably having second thoughts. As an editor she ought to have given him a rundown on what to expect. She owed it to him to make it as easy as possible. A little explanation was only sensible.

"Sensible," she repeated as she started out the door and into the corridor.

"I doubt that," was the caustic reply from the open bedroom door she passed, the room in which Daisy should have been sleeping for hours.

"I can still fire you," she called, and kept going.

The jeer of disbelieving laughter followed her down the stairs.

The night was perfect, velvet black, studded with points of light. The breeze off the Sound, still cool but not unpleasant, ruffled Dan's hair.

Sitting in a deck chair, his legs sprawled out and crossed at the ankles, he seemed not to notice her.

"What's wrong?" she asked softly. "Can't you sleep?"

"No."

"I told you to take the bed."

"Too big for one person alone. I'd get a guilty conscience being so wasteful."

"Somehow it's hard to credit Dan Bailey with a conscience."

"It isn't hard to credit you with one. Is that it? Is it your conscience that's holding you back?"

"Dan, please, I'm not that kind of woman. I mean, it isn't that I wouldn't like to have sex with you. I'm sure I would. But not when I'm working."

"And when aren't you working?"

"Almost never."

"That's what I thought."

They sat in silence for a time, both filled with thoughts of possibilities that were illogical and compelling. Hannah knew that a relationship with a man like Dan would be foolish. He'd be gone by the next weekend. She'd only be hurt if she allowed him to get too close. Her father and her grandfather had taught her about restless men who had to keep moving.

But sitting there, smelling his cologne, listening to him breathe—it all seemed so right, so perfect.

"Hannah?"

"Yes?"

"Nothing."

"No, what? What were you about to ask?"

"Why'd you come down here?"

"Because I wanted—I ought to prepare you for tomorrow. I mean, I don't want to make this any harder on you than it has to be."

He groaned.

"I mean I don't want—"

"Yes you do. You want me as much as I want you."

"That wasn't what I was going to say."

"I know. But you should have. I've spent the last five years working nonstop. My life has been a series of stopovers, beginnings and endings, successes and failures. Until this assignment. Then I had all the time in the world to look at my life and see how little I've accomplished."

"I don't believe that. You've done what you had to do, just as I have. You haven't deliberately hurt people and you haven't done anything illegal."

"How do you know that?"

"I—I just do. What were you hoping to accomplish in prison?"

He thought a moment, then gave her his planned answer. "I was there to do a story on how easy it is for the people who are serving their sentences in a minimum security prison."

"Did you find any problems?"

"No more than I expected. Why?"

"I always wanted to write. But I couldn't do those kinds of stories. They're too painful. I guess I'm more into bringing a little joy into someone's life. I could never be the watchdog for the world."

"I'm not sure how true that is anymore. Our motives have become caught up in our success, and we've become a pack of copycats, more interested in editorializing than reporting the truth. The politicians and financiers control the press, they always have."

"You sound pretty disillusioned."

"I guess I am. I deal with reality and you deal with fantasy, and in the long run we're both doing the same thing."

"Oh? What's that?"

"We're trying to hide ourselves in our work because we can't deal with life on a personal basis."

"Wow! That's pretty potent stuff, Mr. Bailey."

"So are you, Ms. Clendening. And I think you'd better take yourself back up those steps before I get more personal than either of us wants."

"Save it for tomorrow," she said quickly. "Being Razor Cody is more exciting than being a real ex-con, I promise."

"And how is that?"

"Well, for starters, as Razor you fall in love with a beautiful woman."

"That would be the lovely Rachel?"

"Yes. Rachel is the heroine."

"Does she have a big four-poster bed?"

"As a matter of fact, she does."

Oops! Hannah had painted herself into a corner. Did Razor make love to Rachel? Yes, powerfully, beautifully, fantastically. Could she tell Dan? Not if she expected to get back up those stairs alone.

As she started back inside she said, "Maybe you'd better read the book."

"Don't suppose you'd give me a hint, in the interest of proper motivation for the picture."

"Well, I could tell you the name of the book."

"Tell me," he asked.

"It's called *The Morning After*."

"You want me to wear *what*?"

Dan Bailey stood in the hallway in a pair of indecent jeans, legs spread and eyes flashing. If he'd been wearing guns, he'd have drawn one.

"Dan, don't be difficult, please," Hannah was saying. "We will use two scenes in the book. One is very formal. In it you'll be wearing a white dinner jacket and dark pants. The other—"

"The other is a nude scene," Daisy interrupted. "Of course, you don't have to be nude if you don't want to. Razor's body won't be fully displayed. We'll only show from the—ah, hipline up. But you'll have to pose in a bikini."

Dan stared at both women, his scowl changing to a barely restrained grin.

What had he gotten himself into? A long-legged blonde was playing havoc with his body parts by suggesting nude love scenes. And all this was to be recorded by a photographer with only *one* eye. Dan didn't know much about romance covers, but he knew about wild fantasies, and he'd landed flat in the middle of one.

Suddenly he was inspired. "If I have to pose in a bikini, Madam Editor, so do you."

"But Rachel's not in that shot. You and Rachel do the evening-wear scene together. The other features a shot of Razor alone. Just you, Dan, and your tattoo."

"No. If I have to parade around half-naked, I'm going to have some company. Take it off, angel. I'm waiting."

Hannah looked helplessly at Daisy. Will, the photographer, swallowed a laugh and announced that he was ready. He was also on the clock, and Hannah could tell from the set of Dan's jaw that unless she complied, the shoot was going nowhere.

"All right. I'll change. But you'll have to do at least one shot without me in it."

"Only if you do the same."

Hannah gave a shrug of frustration and marched upstairs to her bedroom. She pulled a metallic turquoise bathing suit from her drawer and slipped into it.

Hannah ran a comb through her hair and checked her appearance in the mirror. She should have bought a one-piece suit. This one was too revealing. Normally she paid little attention to the way she looked, but suddenly she felt strange about her body. At the last minute she threw a white lace beach coat over her shoulders and descended the stairs.

Both Will and Dan caught sight of her at the same time. Will let out a whistle of appreciation. Dan only stared.

The models were perfect. The weather agreeable. Dan, resigned to complying with the first few poses, took the positions as if he were a professional. It was only when he insisted on sharing the shot with Hannah that Daisy's dire prediction came true, for everything went downhill from there.

When Daisy had said Dan's physical reaction would be caught by the camera, she'd been more accurate than she knew. The photographer grinned constantly. Daisy flittered about, adjusting, suggesting, enjoying.

Hannah's face flamed.

"Stop this!" she growled as she felt Dan pressing his reaction against her.

"Stop what? I'm new at this, so you'll have to tell me exactly what you want."

"You're enjoying this, Dan Bailey."

"Shouldn't I?"

"No!"

"You mean your regular models don't?"

"Not like this. They've been trained not to respond to the situation."

"Ah, but you didn't want one of them, did you? You wanted a real man, with real feelings, real desires. Didn't you tell me that I'm Razor Cody in the flesh?"

"Well, yes, but I didn't expect—this."

"I know. I do apologize, but I had such trouble resting last night. If I'd had some way to relax, this probably wouldn't be happening."

Daisy, who couldn't help but hear their conversation, chortled. "You could have fooled me!"

"Daisy, my darling. Nobody could ever fool you," Dan said. "But there are situations where better results would be obtained as a result of proper relaxation methods. Would you care to let me demonstrate, Hannah?"

Hannah had tried to maintain her composure. She'd watched models struggle to keep their emotions under control, even when on occasion the male lost it for a moment. It wasn't unheard of, and they simply had the artist correct the situation in the final painting. But this was different. This was personal.

And it was becoming much too volatile. Every time Dan closed his arms around her and pulled her back against his stomach, she felt the sizzle between them, the sizzle and his arousal. In the skimpy suit Daisy had provided for Dan, there was no concealing it, and Dan didn't seem to care.

By this time the photographer obviously sympathized with Dan and began offering suggestions for new and more intimate poses, all in the name of art.

But what was happening wasn't art, it was sex, and Hannah had to take control.

"Mr. Bailey, please come upstairs. I think we need to talk."

"Not me," Dan said, "talk is not going to make things—right."

"No, but a talk will cool things down."

"I doubt it, but I'll give it my best shot."

Dan turned to the photographer and gave a conspiratorial salute. To Daisy it was a knowing wink.

To Hannah it was two arms that captured her as quickly as she closed the door behind them. "What are you doing?" she demanded, but two lips swallowed up her words and turned her protest into a bursting need that drove every rational thought from her mind.

Blindly and irrationally she gave in to the wonderful feelings that came with his touch. Bare skin against bare skin. Parts that fitted together as if they'd been cut from the same fabric sought the spaces where they were meant to rest. And all sense of time and place vanished.

Hannah didn't know how long they'd been kissing when she heard a pounding on the door. "Hannah! Hannah! That's mighty quiet conversation in there. Will's ready to shoot the clinch shots. Hannah!"

It was Dan who drew back, giving Hannah a rueful smile. "Sorry, angel, the warden is signaling lock-down."

"What?" Hannah felt as if she'd been dipped in hot wax and left to dry in the wind.

Daisy knocked again. "I said, let's get the show on the road. Time is money, and I'm thinking that you've lost track of it."

"Yes, thanks, Daisy," she said. "We'll be down right away. Just give us a second."

"If you're sure."

They heard Daisy's irregular steps moving back down the stairs.

"Look—"

"Dan, I—"

"You first," Dan finally said, his back to her now as he looked out the window.

"I don't know what came over me," she answered, "but this can't go on. You're interfering with my business and my life. I can't allow that."

"You're right."

"Let's get the shoot finished, and I'll find you another place to write your story. Maybe there's a spare desk in my office in the city."

"Maybe."

Hannah didn't know why it bothered her so much that he was agreeing. Getting him out of her house and her life was the sensible thing to do, for both of them. She had to read two proposals and finish line editing a manuscript before she took the train into the city the next day. But her suggestion wasn't working out. The words agreed, but the tension in the room overrode the acceptance.

"Why do I get the feeling that you aren't going along with this, Dan?"

"Because it isn't going to work. I knew it the moment I kissed you back at the prison. I knew that we were going to mess up each other's life, and I couldn't see a way in hell to stop it."

"You did?"

"And so did you. But I'm willing to give it a shot if you are. Where's this dinner jacket?"

"In the closet. I'll get dressed in the bathroom and leave the bedroom to you."

"No, I'll take the bathroom. I'll need to shave for the elegant shot, won't I?"

"Yes."

"All right, then." He jerked the hanger from the closet and slammed the door behind him.

But it wasn't all right. They knew it. Daisy knew it the moment she looked at them. And the camera knew it as Will snapped the pictures.

He took shots of them together, two separate shots of Hannah and Dan in their evening wear, then began packing up his cameras and equipment.

"Take care, boss," Daisy whispered as she hugged Hannah good-bye. "This isn't a manuscript and Dan isn't make-believe.

"Can't you stay, Daisy?"

"I don't think so. Be careful, Hannah. Make sure you—never mind. Forget what I said. Write your own script. You've got a real man here. There's not a romance reviewer in the world who wouldn't give this story a gold-star five."

Five

Write her own script? Hannah was an editor, not a writer. She didn't have a clue where to begin. But as an editor she knew that she needed to slow down the action.

"Thank you for going along with the photographer, Dan," she said.

"Thank you for offering me a place to work for a few days."

"It's the least I could do. Are you familiar with the WordStar software?" This was working, she decided, simple conversation, except Dan was looking at the keyboard as if he'd never seen a computer before.

"Yes," he finally answered, "I knew another writer in Paris who used this program."

"Paris?"

And it had been spring and beautiful. The girl, one of many he'd met and loved along the way, was older than he, and very beautiful, and he'd left her without a thought. She'd only been part of the time, his youth, his beginning as a journalist.

"And the writer was a woman?"

"How did you know?"

"Because I hear the pain in your voice. Did something happen?"

"Yes. Not then, but later. She was a reporter too, the one who advised me to do whatever you have to, to get the story."

Dan turned his attention back to the computer, effectively closing the door to the past. And Hannah knew he regretted having let her in that small distance. She could make it easy on him by finding another direction for her attention as well.

"I still have the company car, so I'll be driving into the city in the morning, Dan. You'll have all day alone to work on your story."

"Yeah, sure. I have a couple of things to check out before I begin. Thanks. Is there a local newspaper?"

To Dan, the camaraderie had vanished with the mention of Paris. Their words were stilted now, as if they were strangers. Except strangers hadn't touched intimately. Strangers didn't know the feel of the other's body, the smell of their special fragrances, the acknowledged desire that had flared between them, flared and been tamped down to smolder beneath the awkwardness of small talk.

"Yes, just past the candy store in one of the restored houses. *The Jeffersonian Ledger,* you can't miss it."

"Think they'll have a decent file room?"

"All the way back to the first newspaper in the early eighteen hundreds."

"That old, huh? They don't usually last that long."

"Yes, but it's for sale. So far there hasn't been much interest. Not many people want to operate a small-town newspaper now."

"You know the owner?"

"Very well. He's only had it a couple of years, but he's losing another editor. So far he's held on, but I don't know how long that will last."

"Hmm, maybe I know someone who'd be interested. I'll think about it."

"You take the big bed tonight, Dan. I'll sleep in the little room."

"No, I won't take your room, Hannah."

"They're both my rooms, Dan. One's the before and one's where I sleep now."

He raised his gaze, taking in the soft skin and clear blue eyes. "That's a strange way to put it. The before and the now? What about the after?"

"I'm not there yet. The little room was mine for most of my life. The big one belonged to my grandfather. I haven't changed it any."

"I thought it seemed a bit severe."

"It suits me," she said softly. "Would you like to go for a walk, go down to the village maybe, to get an ice cream?"

"Not one of those flavor-of-the-month parlors?"

"No," she answered, taking a deep breath. "Besides, I think this month's choice has already been made. It's just a matter of deciding whether we share one cone or get separate ones."

"Then I'd love to go."

He was back in the low-slung jeans, boots, and blue shirt. She'd donned blue slacks, a red-and-white blouse with a sailor collar, and canvas shoes. She thought of the comparison and gave a light laugh as she closed and locked the door behind them.

"What's funny?"

She took a measured look at her houseguest. "A sailor and a cowboy. We're a real match, aren't we?"

He didn't even attempt to answer that question. Instead he turned her neatly around, and they started down the street to the village. "Why aren't you married, Hannah?"

"Never been asked."

"I find that hard to believe."

"Believe it. Why aren't you?"

"Never had the time."

That she could believe. From what she'd heard of the infamous Dan Bailey, he moved rapidly across the world from one broken heart to another.

"The truth is, I haven't been asked because I never let a man get close enough. You haven't asked because you've never given yourself time. I think we're both single by choice."

"Or," he said in a low voice, "because we're both scared to death to take a chance on being hurt."

They walked for a time without talking, allowing themselves the luxury of simply being together, holding hands like two normal people, like two lovers who knew that the possibility of a night together still lingered out there before them.

At the foot of the hill was a strip of businesses, art galleries, seafood shacks, open to the air and filled with late-night diners. The ice cream shop where she took him also sold sinfully delicious chocolates and other delicacies, which Dan insisted on sampling.

They settled on separate flavors in a double-cup cone to be shared as they walked along the dock.

He tasted his Rocky Road and held it out, watching her pink tongue flick the strawberry flavor she'd chosen.

"You aren't going to pull that let's-just-be-friends routine, are you, Hannah? Because I haven't been friends with a girl that I wanted to make love to in years. I'm a bit more direct than that now."

It was his turn for a lick.

"Friends are people I can count on, Dan, and I doubt that applies to you. I have the feeling that you'll be gone before I even know where you're from."

She licked, catching a chunk of strawberry between her teeth.

"I'm from Augusta, Georgia," he said. "A long way from Augusta, Georgia, so far that I never want to go back."

"Is there someone waiting for you there?"

"My father, the Honorable Daniel Davis Bailey, is there. My brother, Congressman Robert Revis Bailey, is there, and my mother, Patricia-the-mediator, is there. But whenever I'm around, even she can't keep the peace."

They took a lick at the same time, their noses bumping, their breaths mixing, their pulses fluttering at the nearness.

Hannah shivered and backed away. She missed holding his hand. Even sharing the ice cream cone wasn't the same as touching.

"What about you, Hannah? You live in your grandfather's house. Your mother passed away, Daisy told me. What about your father?"

"He recently remarried. I don't fit in his life any more. The truth is, I never did. Once I figured that out, I stopped trying. Oh, he doesn't ignore me. He just doesn't quite know what to do with a daughter who is as old as his new wife."

"So you cut out?"

"I like to think I gave him space. Which is what he always wanted."

"What about you, Hannah Clendening, what do you want?"

"I don't know exactly. I like my life just the way it is. I suppose that I'll know what I want when I get there."

"So you take in heroes and heroines and people who don't quite fit anywhere else?"

They leaned against the wood railing around the pier while Dan finished the ice cream. He ripped the cone into small pieces and threw them one at a time into the water where two swans were swimming together.

"I don't understand what you mean."

"I mean Daisy, for one. Isn't she a little old to be a trainee?"

"Her husband left her and she needed a job. Besides, she's the best employee I ever had."

"And Will, a photographer with only one eye?"

"The best eye for picture making you'll ever see."

"And me?" he asked, "where do I fit into your group of misfits?"

She turned away from the water and leaned against the rail. "I don't know. I never made room before for anybody like you. This is all virgin territory."

"Virgin?"

She took a deep breath and let it out, pointedly avoiding eye contact. "Almost," she said softly.

The lonely horn of the last ferry from Bridgeport sounded from out in the water. The lights along the shopping strip began to go out, one by one.

"You know they mate for life," he finally said.

"Who?"

"The swans. If one is killed, the other often dies of a broken heart."

"I'm not surprised. I'm just surprised that they ever mate. They must not know the possibilities for being hurt."

"They might be smarter than us. They may believe that the mating is worth the risk."

"I don't think so," she said softly.

"Neither do I," he echoed. But he could wonder.

He'd expected to feel awkwardness when they returned. But there was none. Instead she went about closing up the house as she must have every night, locking the door, opening the windows toward the Sound so that they would get the breeze, and turning out all the lights except a tiny one on the bookshelf beside the fireplace.

"I'll leave this on in case you have an urge to create in the middle of the night," she offered as she headed toward the stairs.

"Thanks."

"Would you like to watch some television?"

"Television?" he repeated, remembering where the television set was and where he'd had to sit to view the screen. "No, I guess not. Would you?"

"Oh. Of course, the set is in your room. Let me get my manuscripts so that I won't disturb you."

"I don't think that's gonna do it," he said with a pained expression, "but we can try."

Hannah's face flushed, and she turned and fled up the stairs. He was right. She'd have to move into the city to quell the disturbance.

Dan followed more slowly, leaning against the door frame as she grabbed the briefcase he'd seen on the back seat of her car. "I have to get something to sleep in." She pulled a sheer red garment from a drawer and mangled it as she clutched it against her abdomen.

"Not on my account," he said. His voice was husky. His eyes were narrowed. "Sleeping garments are one article of clothing I never pack. It's much simpler that way." He took a step forward.

"I've never been considered a simple person." She took a step back. "In fact, if there's a way to complicate things, I do."

"There isn't." He was standing directly in front of her, taking her briefcase and planting it on the floor. Next he rescued the scrap of fabric from her hand and held it up to the light, what there was of it. "A teddy?"

"Only the top half." She felt the bed pressing against the back of her knees. "Please, Dan."

"We left Dan back on the dock. Tonight, Miss Rachel, I'm Razor Cody, and I've come for my revenge."

"But that's only in the book," she managed to say, her emotions so churned that she could barely speak.

"But book characters are the ones you feel most comfortable with, aren't they? I've never been an imaginary lover before."

He placed his hand against her cheek, cupping it gently.

Her body responded instantly, warming to his touch, nerve endings tingling downward like a thousand messengers alerting her to his presence. She felt as if she'd been painted with some kind of electrical conductor that hummed with energy.

Her chin was thrust proudly forward, her knees weakening by the moment, her gaze fixed on the earring which glittered through the thick strands of his hair.

She licked her lips in an attempt to replace the moisture that had evaporated from her mouth. "Why do you wear it?"

"What?"

"The earring?"

"It's been a part of my persona for the last few years. There is a certain mystique attached to a man wearing one, and I've been told it makes me interesting. Do you find me interesting, Miss Rachel?"

"Infinitely, Mr. Cody, but I've read the book. I know something you don't."

His fingers moved down her cheek and along her neck to the collar of the sailor blouse. "Somehow I suspected that. Why don't you give me a quick review."

Write your own script, Daisy had said. For once, Daisy was right. This was her chance to be the author. The hero and heroine were as real as two lovers could be. She had established the premise: two people who were intensely attracted to each other and had no time for a serious relationship. The only thing she didn't know yet was the plot. But her best authors often told her that their most exciting books were the ones where the characters were turned loose to find their own way.

The prison had been the opening scene. The photographic shoot the hook. Now came the climactic moment. Except her calm analysis went straight out the window when his fingers found the buttons of her blouse and began to unfasten them.

Hannah stayed his hand for a moment while she moved to the bedside table and turned out the lamp. Then she was sorry she had. As long as they'd been touching, the force field had short-circuited any reservations. Now a wave of uncertainty swept over her.

As if he understood, Dan said, "Hannah, I don't want to rush you. I know how I feel, but I can wait." He forced himself to turn his back and walk over to the telescope and adjust the setting so that he could see. "Do you study the stars?"

"Study them? No," she said, joining him at the

window. "My grandfather did. I enjoy looking. They're constant. I like knowing that the same lights I'm seeing will be seen for millions of years. They're like promises kept."

"And that's important to you, keeping promises."

Her simple "Yes" said it all. She'd been disappointed by someone she cared about, and that broken promise had fed her ambition. He let out a deep sigh of regret, knowing that even though he could touch her and take them back to where they'd been, he wouldn't.

Dan Bailey had been a lot of things in his life, but he wouldn't be a broken promise.

Not this time.

"Don't worry, Hannah. I don't have to read the book to know that Miss Rachel was a prize worth treasuring. Dan Bailey might be a rogue in real life, but for once he's going to act like a hero."

"You know you don't have to be noble," she said softly. "I rather think I'm learning to like you as a maverick."

"I know, and I like you, too much. I'm trying to make a sacrifice here, and it scares the hell out of me."

"I think you're fooling yourself, Dan. I think you're much more heroic than you want people to know."

"Sure. My mother would be proud of me."

"And your father too, I think."

"No, my father never approved of anything I attempted. The sanctimonious old boy would probably laugh out loud at what I'm doing now."

"Then I pity him for what he's missed."

"Good night, Miss Rachel. Dan Bailey regrets that he won't share Razor Cody's morning after."

Dan gave Hannah a light kiss and turned away, feeling very sanctimonious and totally frustrated.

"Oh, Dan, look."

He moved back beside her, casting his gaze to the heavens.

"A falling star," she whispered. "Oh, no!"

Before he understood what was happening she had buried her face against his shoulder. "Nothing is constant, Dan. No matter how much we want it to be. Nothing in the world. All we have is the moment, this moment."

She kissed him. He could never say that he'd been the one to take advantage of her. It was the exact opposite. She stood on tiptoe and pressed her lips against his, filled with the sweet pain of uncertainty.

"Don't do this, Hannah. I'm not sure how noble I can be."

"I don't want you to be noble, Dan. I'm very tired of being alone. I want to be with the bad-boy reporter. It's time I learned about making love with a real man."

Her lips were parted and being rimmed impatiently by her tongue. Her blouse was half open, her breasts were pressing against his bare chest, and her thighs were melded to his.

He pulled away, removed his boots, then moved close to her and ripped off his shirt. She let her blouse slide from her shoulders and fall to the floor. All the time their lips were poised, room between only for breath. And then they were kissing each other, wildly, fiercely, possessively.

His hand slid down her back, pausing in the hollow between the pockets of her slacks, pulling her against him. She gave a little moan and burrowed closer.

It was all he'd been afraid that it would be, and more.

For Hannah, they were riding the comet, ready to reach the stars. And all those times she'd advised her writers that the first love scene was happening too soon simply vanished in the stardust that was stinging her body with fire.

"Sorry, guys," she whispered as she felt him strip her slacks and underwear from her body. "If I'd known how it really was, I'd never have made them wait."

"Are we talking heroes of the month, here?" he asked as he unzipped his jeans and stepped out of them.

"Yes, as an editor, I've done them a great injustice."

"As their real-life representative, I'll be happy to help you make amends."

"Don't talk to me, Dan. I've heard enough words to last forever. I just want to feel."

With a growl of sheer animal pleasure he lifted her and carried her to the bed, placing her on the pillows and lying beside her. There were no more words, only touch and taste and the sheer exhilaration of two people whose responses fed and built on the other's. Where hands led, lips followed. Where calm was involved, nerve endings rebelled and movement came alive.

Dan drew away, his gaze slowly sweeping her body in the darkness. The light of the moon, the lover's moon, showered the bed with silver, turning her hair into pure enchantment. "Do you know how very beautiful you are?" he murmured.

"Only for you."

She felt his muscles coil and tighten as he raised himself on one arm, allowing his free hand to range across her breasts and down her stomach, where his fingers curled around the hair now moistened with the evidence of her desire.

"Is it true? You've never been with a man before?"

She gave a hesitant smile and answered honestly. "Been with a man? Yes. Once there was a man, but it didn't work out. We had sex, but I've never had a man make love to me."

"Wait!"

He lifted himself and moved through the darkness to plunder through his jeans, pulling something from his wallet.

"What are you doing?"

"I'm taking care of you," he whispered as he moved over her. "Know me. Feel what you've done to me, Hannah, my darling."

She shivered, the involuntary movement of her body responding to the heat of his presence.

"Ah, Hannah, beautiful Hannah. I'm sorry. I can't stop the words. They're part of what I feel, of the spell you've cast over me."

He was sliding himself up and down, nipping at

her breasts on the downward movement and her lips as he slipped up again.

Dimly she was aware of his words, of his concern, of his holding back. But the fire that he'd stoked to full flame was driving her to the brink of madness.

And then he was inside her. She gasped, arching herself to take even more of him, sheathing him with her liquid heat.

Higher and higher they climbed, until they exploded into a place that was beyond anything she'd ever dreamed.

She cried out, awash in the sensation of what he was doing to her. For one night she'd crossed over into the realm of fantasy that until now she'd only read about.

But written words were only puny reflections of the truth. All the fantasies paled in comparison to this man and this night.

Hannah sighed. She felt as if her bones had turned to liquid, that she and Dan had somehow become one being.

And then he rolled over, pulling her with him, spreading her legs so that one was along his thigh and the other across him, leaving that part of her that still throbbed pressed against his hip.

"Oh, Dan. Oh, Dan," she whispered over and over again.

There was no comprehending what had happened, just the floating sensation of satisfaction. Hannah deliberately refused to allow her mind to focus on anything beyond the man and the moment.

"Miss Rachel Kimbel has been very naughty," she said with a smile as she closed her eyes. "And she wouldn't change a thing if she could. I wonder if the author knows?"

"Razor Cody agrees, and he thinks there is something to be said for repetition—for effect, of course."

"Of course," Hannah agreed, running her fingertips across his chest. "A good editor never stifles an author's creativity, nor the characters'."

"And you, my darling Hannah, fulfill every writer's wish, an editor who doesn't rewrite the story."

"Not when I have a gold-star five."

Dan was gone the next morning when Hannah awoke. The bed covers were rumpled. The smell of lovemaking was caught up in the sheets.

Hannah stretched, caught sight of the clock on the night table, and groaned. She was late. She was very late, and she hadn't even looked at the proposals she'd promised to have an answer on.

"So fire me," she said, turning on the shower. Everybody's entitled to goof off when they meet the man of their dreams, the man who—She cut that sentence off because the rest of it involved falling in love, and that was forbidden territory.

Ten minutes later she'd donned her walking shoes, crammed her smart black pumps into her briefcase, and threaded her arms into the black-checked jacket of her newest power suit.

On the stove she found a pot of coffee on Warm. A half-filled cup was resting on the desk beside the computer, along with a couple of crumpled pages of copy. But no Dan. Stepping onto the deck, she shaded her eyes from the bright fall sunshine and searched the area around the harbor. And then she spotted him, the lone figure walking along the water, hands in his pockets, shoulders rounded in dejection or contemplation.

She hadn't thought about what had happened from his point of view, or what would happen next. But from the look of her desk, it wasn't that easy for Dan. Either their sleeping together had left him with doubts, or his article wasn't going well.

In either case he'd chosen to be miserable alone instead of sharing it with her. That didn't surprise her. She kept her feelings to herself, too, so much so that her friends thought she never had a dark moment. Fighting back the urge to follow him, she wrote a brief note explaining where a spare key was and her phone number in case he needed something.

She resisted the temptation to read what he was writing. He expected her to be gone for the day. Maybe that was best. What would she have said if she had called out to him?

No, it was better to get her life back to normal. Bad Boy Bailey was a temporary fixture in her life, just passing through, and she couldn't afford to begin thinking of him as permanent.

Even if the idea was appealing.

Get real, Hannah, she chided herself. Dan is purely fiction. As long as you remember that, you'll be okay. You'll get to the end of the story and be sad that it's over, just like any other good romance. This is your script and you're the heroine. Ask yourself the question you ask about all heroines. What do you want more than anything?

She got into the company car and started the engine. Backing down the drive, she thought about what she'd done and smiled. For the first time since she'd moved back into her grandfather's house, she'd left it unlocked.

What she wanted, she decided as she listened to the singing of her heart, was for Dan to be there when she returned. It was too soon for a bleak moment. She'd write her scenes one day at a time, treasure them, and store them up as a special memory.

A memory was a kind of promise, wasn't it? A promise that had once been kept.

Six

"Sorry, guys, I'm late. I didn't get my manuscript edited or the proposals read, and I haven't got your art and marketing information ready. I'll get it all done tonight. I promise."

To her credit, Daisy didn't say a word. Neither did Herb, the art director, Tom, the marketing director, nor Bets, the secretary who doubled as a first reader. The ten o'clock meeting had been delayed until eleven with no explanation. Now there was no hiding the twitching of lips as the editorial staff tried to pretend they hadn't been told about Hannah's newest hunk.

"About the cover for *The Morning After*. As you probably know, I found the model we're using for Razor." She glanced at Herb.

"Yes, we heard," Herb said noncommittally. "Daisy says he's 'spectacular.' If he satisfies you, he'll satisfy me."

Hannah swallowed hard. For a moment her throat became completely closed off and she couldn't breathe. Satisfy? There was no way she could touch that comment and maintain any semblance of order.

Neither could Daisy. Unable to hold back any longer, she gave up and giggled.

Uncertain about what was happening, Bets looked up in confusion. "Did I miss something?"

"I'll say," Daisy quipped.

Hannah cleared her throat, literally forcing air into her lungs. "All right, simmer down. I suppose I can assume that Daisy has shared the details of my weekend with you, Herb?"

"Well, not the details, but she did hit the high spots. I'm willing to listen to any intimate revelations you'd care to share."

"I'll bet you are. But there aren't any. And if there were, I wouldn't share them. The model prefers to remain anonymous, and I intend to see that his request is honored. He's promised to be available until we see the prints and have what we need. Has anyone heard from Will yet?"

"Not yet," Bets said.

"Fine, let's talk about the sales figures." She was about to turn the discussion over to Tom when there was a knock on the door, followed by the receptionist, who waited for permission to speak.

"What?" Hannah barked, uncharacteristically loud for her. "What?"

"I'm sorry, but there's a man named Dan on the phone. He says he's—staying at your house?"

"Dan?" Hannah stood, hoping beyond hope that

her eagerness didn't show on her face. Though she knew that was useless. Every person around that table knew the cardinal rule: Nobody interrupted an editorial meeting, under threat of death.

"Yes, of course. Excuse me. I mean I'd better. He—"

"Go," Daisy said. "We don't need you to talk about how we're going to catch up on the backlog. We'll just go through the motions like we always do."

Hannah ducked out of the conference room, headed for her tiny office, and closed the door. She took a deep breath before lifting the receiver. "Hannah Clendening speaking."

"Hello—Am I interrupting?"

"Oh, no. Not at all," she lied, desperately fighting the urge to slide down behind her desk and cradle the phone against her ear. "Is something wrong?"

"Probably, but that's not why I called. I—we've been invited out to dinner."

"We have? By whom?"

"I walked down to the newspaper to take a look at their morgue, and the man who's filling in started talking about the paper. I asked a few questions. You know, in case I hear of an interested buyer, and the editor mentioned that he was having dinner with the owner. He suggested that I come along."

"Dinner with the owner of the newspaper?" Hannah hoped the panic in her voice didn't show. She hadn't been entirely honest with Dan. The owner of her company, C. C. Lowen, was also Carl Lowenstein, owner of the local newspaper— and her father.

"Why would you want to do that?" she asked weakly.

"I've heard a lot about Carl Lowenstein, but he's such a recluse, I've never met him. I'm a reporter, remember, and I smell a story."

That was what she was afraid of. She'd never consciously concealed her relationship with her father, but for so many years he'd ignored her that she still wasn't completely comfortable with being Carl Lowenstein's daughter. She ought to tell Dan, but it was hard.

"He's sending a car, and if you come with me, you'll be my cover. I mean, who's to know that we aren't just friends?"

"Nobody, except our host. You see, Carl—"

"Our host doesn't even know you," Dan cut her off. "This is just a social occasion, unless you have an objection."

"Me? Ah, no. No objection. But you told me that you could never be friends with a woman you wanted to make love to. Have you changed your mind?"

"About making love to you? Not on your life. If you hadn't had to work today, I'd never have let you out of the house."

"Oh, I wondered where you were when I got up."

"Forcing myself to give you a little space, angel."

"So we can be lovers, but you're still not sure about being friends." Hannah could almost feel the warmth of his breath as he spoke. His voice was low and intimate, filled with the kind of sensuality that she hadn't heard since she was sixteen and had listened in on her father's telephone calls.

"No," he answered. "But someone once told me that a good journalist always keeps an open mind."

"Someone in Paris?"

"No, someone back home in Augusta. That was when I was rebelling over going to law school as my father wanted."

"Your mother?"

"No, not my mother. She always agreed with my father. It was Mattie, and she hadn't been talking about reporting back then. She was talking about families and tolerance of people who love you."

"Mattie? Was she a girlfriend too?"

"Not exactly, but she was the first woman who ever really loved me. She was our family cook. I'd better let you get back to work. Mr. Lowenstein's driver will pick us up about six-thirty. Is that too early?"

"No. That'll be fine." If she worked through lunch and left an hour early. Which should go over real well, since she'd been an hour late to work. Avoiding the rush-hour traffic and taking the train would put her in Port Jefferson by six—if it was on time. If not—she didn't want to think about that, or the fresh smirks on the faces of her editorial staff.

Mercifully, Will had come in with the prints. He'd pinned them on the viewing board, and the staff was staring spellbound at the results.

"What's wrong?" Hannah pushed her conversation with Dan to the back of her mind. The kind of dead silence she was hearing could only mean total disaster. "If the photos are bad, we can reshoot them. I'm sure once he gets loosened up, he'll be able to give us what we want."

"Hannah, if this man gives us any more, the book will incinerate before the owner gets it out of the store. Take a look."

They formed a path directing her attention to the picture board, to the dark-haired man in the bikini and the woman he was focused on. There were two shots: one from the side and one of the front. In the front view her head was tilted up, and she was gazing at him with total adoration, shared adoration, almost as if their eyes were connected by some invisible band.

The side view, well, it didn't matter that he didn't bother to hide his arousal. It didn't matter that they were posing for a camera. Any person looking at the pair was automatically caught up in the intensity of their longing, the passion, the electricity between them.

"It's the damndest thing I ever saw," Will was saying. "You could even see it on the negative."

"What?" Hannah whispered, allowing her gaze to slide across the other prints.

"Aura. There's a theory that plants and animals, including humans, produce an electromagnetic field called aura. The color of a person's aura is determined by the state of their emotions. As you can see, the aura here is intense. I don't have to tell you that it's hot."

"Will, how'd you do it?" Hannah was stunned. In every picture, both she and Dan seemed surrounded by a shimmering cloud of red-orange color. "Is something wrong with the camera?"

"Nope. I used it again last night, and those pictures didn't come out X-rated."

Hugh pursed his lips. "Well, you can't blame the man for his reaction. It happens, even to professionals occasionally. Too bad we can't put these exact pictures on the cover."

"Yes," Daisy agreed, "what a shame."

"We'll reshoot," Hannah finally said.

"Not on your life," Herb argued. "I'm the art director. I only wish I were good enough to paint those expressions on canvas. Don't suppose you'd like to go with straight photographs on these books, would you?"

"No, I don't think so," Hannah answered. But she couldn't be sure that what she'd said made any sense. It was difficult to carry on any rational conversation at all.

Nobody mentioned Hannah's presence in the pictures, nor did they verbalize what they all had to be thinking: Hannah looked as if she'd been rolled in firedust and caught in its force field.

Finally she asked, "Which shot for the cover, Herb?"

"It doesn't matter. I could use any one of them. The man is terrific, but I'd like to compliment Miss Rachel Kimbel as well. She's pure dynamite. Wow! She may not be satisfied with Razor, but I am."

"Rachel is satisfied," Hannah whispered under her breath. Or she had been the previous night. *After looking at those pictures, I'm not certain that's true anymore.*

If the train had had an aura, it would have been black, for it was agonizingly slow, arriving in Port

Jefferson at 6:20. By the time Hannah made it home, the limo was waiting in the drive.

Darn! She'd hoped to get there in time to warn Dan about what was going to happen. As it was, she waved at Dan, who was talking to the driver on the deck, dashed up the stairs, and quickly traded her sneakers and power suit for a simple pink dinner dress and heels.

When she came back down the stairs, Dan met her at the bottom. The newspaper wasn't the only place Dan had been. She didn't think that duffel bag had contained gray slacks, a navy jacket, and Italian loafers. Her long-haired man of the earth looked like a million dollars—a wicked million dollars.

While she'd applied her makeup, Hannah had rehearsed what she'd say in the limo. She never counted on her thoughts being scrambled by the intimate kiss Dan gave her on the way out the door.

Once inside the limo, Dan lifted her legs across his body and pulled her into his arms, his fingertips memorizing her bare shoulders, all the while continuing his conversation with the driver about the coming World Series.

She knew nobody could see his hand slide beneath her skirt, but her sudden gasp was obvious. She buried her face against the side of his, whispering in his ear, "What are you doing, Dan Bailey?"

"Doing?" His *too* innocent expression wouldn't have fooled anybody. "Is something wrong?"

"Close the panel, Dan!"

"Sure. Sorry, old boy, my lady wants a little privacy." The panel slid closed, as did Hannah's eyes when Dan swung his legs to the bed-length seat, carrying her with him. "Lord, you taste good!"

"Wait, Dan," she said with a gasp. "We have to talk."

"No words, remember, only feelings. And you feel wonderful. What's this called?"

He'd captured a swatch of the sheer pink fabric of her dress, captured it by pulling the skirt up over her back as he caressed her bottom intimately.

"Dan!" Hannah tried to talk to him, she really did, but her words got lost in the kisses and her resistance got swallowed by the fire.

He didn't make love to her in the car, but it might have been better if he had. When the driver arrived at their destination, Hannah felt as if she'd landed in a bed of fire ants, and, she thought with breathless chagrin, he'd been right. There'd been no conversation at all.

"Now look what you've done," she said, dragging air into her lungs. "I'm a mess."

"You're beautiful. You look thoroughly kissed and—" Dan lost the words. *Wanton. Provocative. Sultry. Desirable. Innocent.* He was a writer, and this time he couldn't begin to come up with the words to capture what he was seeing. Hannah was so completely compelling that Dan was tempted to tell the driver to keep going.

Instead he took a deep breath. Being late might not be smart, and making love to Hannah wasn't something he wanted to rush.

"You're right. The only deal our host will be will-ing to talk about is how to steal my woman. Let's sit and think about the arctic for a while."

"The arctic?"

"As a matter of fact, I'll get out and let you con-jure up your own ice storms. Join me when you're ready." Dan straightened his trousers and got out of the car, asking the driver another question about baseball.

Inside the limo, Hannah fished in her tiny bag and located her lipstick. She applied a fresh coat, ran her fingers through her tousled hair, and decided that they weren't going to fool anybody. Besides, what was about to happen would dampen her emotions, and she wouldn't need polar bears and snowstorms.

She wasn't looking forward to the evening. If Dan hadn't arranged the dinner, she wouldn't have come. She'd met Carl Lowenstein's previ-ous wives, but this last marriage was only three months old and so far she'd managed to avoid the new bride. It was getting harder and harder to watch a man keep marrying women younger than his own child.

Dan was wiping the lipstick from his mouth and straightening his shirt. He took one look at Hannah and decided that the arctic wasn't cold enough. The door to the mansion opened, and a woman wear-ing a black uniform and white apron stood in the entranceway.

"Come in. Mr. Lowenstein is waiting in his study. You'll be dining alone. The other gentleman from the paper has been detained."

"Dan," Hannah whispered under her breath as he took her elbow and directed her inside the house. "About Mr. Lowenstein, you ought to know—"

"No, don't tell me. I like to form my own opinions. That's crucial here. I know enough for now."

"But—"

The study door opened and the silver-haired man moving toward them stopped, looked from Hannah to Dan and back. "Welcome, Dan. Good evening, Hannah. This is a pleasant surprise. I wasn't expecting you."

Dan cut his eyes to Hannah, curious about the undertones in the exchange. "You know Hannah?"

"Dan," Hannah said, straightening her shoulders perceptibly, "I'd like you to meet my father, Carl Lowenstein, known to the publishing world as C. C. Lowen."

"Your father?"

"Of course. I can't imagine why she didn't tell you," Carl said, drawing Hannah and Dan inside the room. "Come and meet my wife, Gina." He turned and held out his hand to the short, plump woman standing by the fireplace.

"Gina, this is my daughter, Hannah, and Dan Bailey, one of the world's foremost journalists."

"Welcome, Dan. I'm so glad to finally meet you, Hannah. Carl has told me so much about you."

"You're Carl's wife?"

Even Dan couldn't miss the surprise in Hannah's voice.

"Yes. Hard to believe, isn't it? I mean I'm not young and beautiful, am I?"

"No—I mean, yes, I'm surprised. You're not what I expected. I mean the others—"

"Were all young enough to be my daughter," Carl said, slipping his arm affectionately around Gina. "Gina is a wife, my wife, not an amusement. Come in, Dan. What can I get you to drink?"

"Yes, darling, do fix Dan a drink while Hannah and I go powder our noses."

Gina's dress was simple. It wasn't even expensive. And she didn't seem impressed with her surroundings or make silly conversation. Hannah followed her automatically, her mind still trying to fathom what she was seeing. Since her mother's death her father had been married three other times. Each new wife had been exactly like the last—leggy, young, and brainless. Hannah couldn't even remember their names.

But Gina was motherly—wifely.

"Your Dan is very handsome," Gina commented as they entered the powder room off the foyer. "I think Carl must have looked a lot like him when he was young, don't you?"

"I don't know. I don't remember seeing him much."

"And there's something about you. In your eyes and your coloring."

"What do you mean?"

"Look in the mirror, Hannah. You're radiant."

Hannah glanced into the mirror and gasped. Gina was right. She was vibrant. She was seeing Miss Rachel Kimbel staring back at her, eyes sparkling, cheeks flushed, hair tousled. She looked as if she'd just come from a man's bed.

"You remind me of me, the first night Carl took me home. I'm afraid I behaved rather shamelessly. I was certain that he'd never want to see me again."

"Shamelessly?" Hannah felt like a parrot.

"Yes, we met on the beach. We walked for hours, and talked. He asked me to dinner that night. When I accepted, I didn't know his name, or that he was"—she looked around—"wealthy. Then he came for me in a limo and I was speechless. It didn't matter, because he wouldn't have listened anyway. He kept kissing me until even I didn't know what I was doing. Can you imagine two sixty-year-olds making out in that room-on-wheels we ride in?"

Hannah couldn't believe her father had even noticed Gina. Yet there was something special about her, something about the direct, down-to-earth honesty of her conversation that was very comforting.

"Of course I drew the line at sleeping with him. I'd slept with only one man in my life, and I was married to him for twenty-five years. When I turned Carl down, he proposed on the spot."

Hannah let out a genuine laugh. "You turned down C. C. Lowen? I bet you were the first person ever to say no to him."

"No, I think you were."

That comment stopped Hannah cold. She'd always avoided personal contact with her father. They'd never treated each other like father and daughter, and C.C. always worked through representatives, even when he offered her the opportunity to create her own line of romance novels.

They were already accustomed to keeping their relationship strictly professional, and once Fantasy Romances became a reality, they simply continued along the same lines.

Both preferred it that way.

But Gina's statement was a genuine puzzle. "I turned him down?"

"Didn't you? I'm sorry. That's what he said. I was repeating what I've been told. He said that when your mother died, he didn't know how to be a father and he left you with your grandparents. Then, later on, you didn't want him. All he could do was stay in the background. When your grandparents died, you wanted to go to boarding school. If I've offended you, I'm sorry."

"No—no," she said, still bewildered by the turn of events. C.C. Lowen didn't know how to do something? That never stopped him from attempting. No, Gina was wrong. Carl had left her with her grandparents, and he hadn't come back for her for years. When he had, Hannah had declined. Her life hadn't been particularly happy, but it had been stable. "You just see a different man from the one I know."

"Tell me about Dan. Is he special?"

"I'm not sure yet. We've only just met."

"Well, I suppose you're stronger than I am at fighting the inevitable. I folded the first night."

"But C.C. proposed."

"It didn't take me long to learn that I was the fifth woman to accept. But that didn't seem to matter. It still doesn't."

"He does seem to be—happy. I wouldn't have thought it."

"I know. It's a surprise, even to me. I had a happy marriage, but loving your father is beyond description. It's like a fairy tale, like one of those books you publish. If that's what you have with Dan, don't hold back. People don't get those kinds of relationships but once in a lifetime."

"I'm not sure I believe in fairy tales."

"But you believe in love. At least you're being offered a chance at it. No one who's experienced it could mistake the connection between the two of you. Now, we'd better get you back before Dan comes after you. He was shooting daggers at me when I whisked you away."

"He was? I didn't notice."

"I suppose you didn't notice the pride in your father's eyes either?"

"No, I guess I didn't."

Hannah allowed herself to be led back to the study without ever having powdered her nose.

"Hannah, your father is telling me how successful your company has become." Dan was standing beside her again, taking her hand in his, holding her possessively.

"I suppose we've done well."

"How are the anniversary-issue specials coming along?" Carl asked.

"They're going to knock your socks off, C.C. I saw the photographs this morning, Dan."

"Oh? And were they what you expected?"

Expected? No, they were more. Simply remembering them brought a blush to her face. She could feel it, but she couldn't stop. It didn't help that there was a very knowing look in Dan's eyes. "They're very powerful, very exciting."

"So was the model," he said.

"It showed."

"Sorry."

"I'm not," she admitted shyly. They were staring at each other, carrying on a conversation as if they were the only two people in the room. "He gave more than I'd hoped for."

"But less than he is capable of, I promise."

"Then I guess I'll have to use him again."

"He—he's more than willing."

"Carl, do you get the feeling that we're in the way here?" Gina gave her husband a hug and focused her bright eyes on him.

"Somebody is," he said, and directed her out of the room and onto the veranda. "You two take all the time you want. Dinner isn't for half an hour. I think Gina and I will take a little stroll."

"They don't even hear you, Carl."

"I'm having a bit of trouble here myself, darling."

"Dan, you have to stop kissing me. We're behaving shamelessly."

"Shamelessly? Ah, angel, what kind of word is that?" He'd switched out the light and lifted her to sit on the edge of the enormous oak desk in the dark corner of the study. Now he was rhythmically pressing himself between her legs.

She would have answered if she could have forced the words past the tightening of her throat—

if Dan hadn't slid his hands beneath her dress and pulled her panties aside so that he could touch her—if he hadn't unzipped his trousers and freed his erection to find the place he was touching. By that time it was much too late for words, for anything except the frantic twitching of nerve endings that ignited and exploded in instant fire.

Moments later she collapsed against him, spent, stunned, and still repeating the phrase. "Shameless."

Gina might not have slept with Carl, but Hannah had no doubt she and her new stepmother had both felt the earth move. Still floating in a state of euphoria, she felt Dan pull away.

"Damn! You've got me acting like some kind of randy schoolboy. Do you realize that I just made love to you right here in the middle of your father's study?"

"I believe I do," she murmured, and gave a satisfied sigh. "Razor Cody is completely shameless!"

"Suppose someone had come in?"

"Nobody did. Gina saw to that."

"But it isn't like me to lose control."

"I know. Me either." She caught his face and drew it down for a gentle, lingering kiss.

"I guess that's what happens when fantasy heroes and heroines meet."

"I don't know about that," Hannah said dreamily. "You're the first real-life hero I ever met."

"I'm no hero, darling. Remember? I'm an ex-con, a dirt-breathing man of the earth."

"And, just like Daisy said, 'utterly gorgeous.' "

Seven

"Don't you ever get tired of the travel, Dan?" Gina asked curiously.

"Sure. Sometimes I have to look at the telephone directory to find out what city I'm in. But usually I'm so involved in what I'm doing that it doesn't matter."

"Like my daughter," Carl commented dryly.

"I don't travel," Hannah said.

"But you're usually so involved in what you're doing that you could be on Mars and you wouldn't know the difference."

Dan finished his coffee and looked at Hannah. "Mars. That's an interesting thought. Have you considered an alien as your flavor of the month?"

"Flavor of the month? You mean as in ice cream?" Gina asked in a puzzled voice.

"Something like that," Dan said, his lips curling for a moment at the corners before he realized what he was doing and made a conscious effort to straighten them.

Once more Hannah realized how seldom Dan took part in simple conversation without any purpose. As for joking, she doubted that he ever indulged in nonproductive nonsense.

"Except," he went on, "Hannah calls them her hunk of the month. They're all temporary, including me."

Gina shook her head. "Somehow I don't think you're temporary."

"I don't know," Carl argued, "Hannah is a contradiction. She's never had much use for the real world. When she was a child she hid out in her room with her books. Never asked for anything, never got dirty, never got into trouble, as if she didn't need anything or anybody."

"Nothing like me," Dan commented. "I don't hide. When I need something, I find a way to get it, or somebody to get it for me. I refuse to believe that Hannah isn't the same too. I'm living proof of that."

"Maybe," Carl pursed his lips in thought, "but up to now what she's done is never for herself. She only deals with the people in her books."

"And what do you call Dan?" Gina asked.

Carl studied Dan for a moment. "I don't know whether Dan is real or a fantasy, but I'm not sure it matters."

"I don't suppose you'd like to stop talking about me as if I weren't here?" Hannah asked with an exaggerated pout to her lower lip.

"She's right," Gina agreed, rising quickly and moving to Hannah's side, where she slipped her arm around her stepdaughter's waist. "Hannah knows what she's doing. Besides, women have a way of recognizing what they want when it comes along, and getting it."

"That's the truth," Carl agreed.

"Maybe some people are happy with their lives as they are?" Hannah said.

Dan looked at Hannah. "And maybe they find that what they have isn't enough; they need something or someone and they have to go after it."

The conversation was becoming too intense for Hannah. She knew Dan was a man who went after what he wanted, but she couldn't figure out why he'd sought out her father. Carl's reclusive ways really didn't make for a very exciting story. And clearly Dan hadn't known that she was Carl's daughter. But the way Dan was staring at her was making her uncomfortable. Coming there had been a mistake, but she hadn't known how to avoid it without disappointing Dan.

"What are your plans now, Dan?" her father was asking.

"Maybe we could talk about that. I'd appreciate some advice from a man who has a better perspective."

"Me? How can I help?"

"You have something I want. I've come to pick your brain and do a little bargaining."

Hannah listened in horror. She'd been wrong. Dan had said he smelled a story. Maybe he hadn't known who she was, but he'd found out. She'd known Dan's reputation for manipulating people to get his stories; that's what had propelled him to the top. Somehow he'd used her to get to her father. It wouldn't be the first time. She'd been a diversion. She felt used.

"Excuse me," she interrupted, "I seem to have developed a headache, Dan. You don't need me any longer. I'll have C.C.'s driver take me home."

Dan gave her an odd look and started toward her. "If you don't feel well, I'll take you home."

That was the last thing she wanted. Her head really was pounding. She couldn't think and couldn't face her father. She had to get away before she made a fool of herself. "No! I mean, you stay and do whatever you came for."

"Let me get you something for your head, Hannah," Gina said.

"No, really." She had to get out of her father's house. It was happening again, as it had on the few occasions when she'd found out that she'd been used to get to her father.

Except for Fantasy Romances, where she earned what she took, she'd kept their relationship on a businesslike level. But this was personal. In her house, Dan was hers. Here, he was a famous journalist, as important and powerful as her father, and she didn't know how to deal with that.

"I have to read some proposals anyway. I've put them off for two days, and I can't delay them any longer. Thank you for the dinner, Gina. I'm very glad you're in the family."

Thirty minutes later, over Gina's protests and Dan's puzzled expression, Hannah was back in her own house. But she couldn't concentrate. She couldn't erase Dan's face from her mind. He'd glared at her first in disbelief, then in silent anger. But he hadn't argued and he hadn't insisted on accompanying her. Just as she'd thought, talking with Carl Lowenstein was more important than being with Hannah Clendening. She didn't know why that hurt so badly, but it did.

She pretended to be asleep when Dan came in. She lay in the darkness in her little bed, listening to him moving about the house. She heard the stairs creak as he came up, the water run as he took a shower, the bed across the hall sag as he sat down on it.

And through every sound and motion, she felt his presence, or the absence of it. The manuscripts lay beside her on the nightstand. She'd finally given up on making any sense out of them and turned off the light. But there was no sleep, only tension that seemed to grow with every second.

Her relationship with Dan was very tenuous, with her father even more so. But she wasn't a little girl any longer. She was a woman, and she had to find a way to face both men as their equal.

Suddenly the door flew open and Dan was silhouetted there. "Dammit, Hannah, why did you leave?"

"I don't know why it matters. You wanted to meet my father. You did."

"Oh, I see. You thought I was using you to get to Carl?"

"Weren't you? I trust you got whatever it was you wanted."

"What I wanted was information. And yes, I got it.

What I want now is you. You don't belong in here. I can't sleep across the hall from you. I can't sleep at all. I don't know why you tore out of there like a bat out of hell, but you're driving me crazy! Do you have a problem with what I'm doing?"

He didn't give her time to answer. Instead he scooped her up in his arms, assaulting her mouth hungrily as he carried her into the big bedroom and fell into bed with her.

"I can't think. I can't work. Every moment I'm not with you is wasted because I can't concentrate anyway. What have you done to me with your fantasies and fairyland?"

She gasped. "I don't know, Dan. I'm having the same problem. Why did you go to talk with my father?"

"I wanted to find out about his newspaper. I had a foolish idea that I—well, never mind. I decided to drop the idea. And why did you tear out of there like a malfunctioning rocket?"

"I guess it was seeing you with C.C. You are so much alike, both strong, powerful, determined. I never could stand up to him, and suddenly I felt that way about you."

"That I'm like your father? I'm not. At least I don't feel very fatherly right now."

"And I don't feel very confident. I haven't accomplished anything since I met you. At home I can't read manuscripts. They all seem silly when I think of you and real"—she didn't say love, but the word was there, unbidden and insistent—"relationships. I might as well not have been in the office, because all I thought about was being here."

They made love—no, not love. They took each other roughly, with savage force and unleashed passion. Afterward they lay in each other's arms, spent and silent.

"I don't know that I can go on like this," Hannah finally said. "My job has been my entire life. Now, suddenly, I can't even read a proposal. Maybe you'd better go."

"I don't know that I can. I think we'll have to ride out the storm."

"You said that you knew in the beginning that we'd destroy each other. I didn't believe you, Dan. Now I'm not so sure. Is it always like this for you?"

His hand, resting on her breast, was warm and possessive. Even relaxed, it claimed and controlled. Even sated with the afterglow of their lovemaking, Hannah felt her skin blaze beneath his touch.

"I don't know," Dan finally answered. "I've been attracted to a lot of women in my life, but this is different. What we have is too intense, too overpowering. If I believed in witchcraft, I'd think you'd cast a spell on me. What about you?"

"I don't know either. I have nothing to compare us with. I've never had time for men. This is all new, but it seems pretty powerful."

They made love for most of the night. When she left the next morning, Dan was still sleeping. Hannah napped on the train instead of reading proposals as she'd planned. When she reached the office, she was still tired and, what was rare for her, grouchy.

"Can we assume that our illustrious leader had

a bad night?" Daisy asked. "Or," she looked at Hannah shrewdly, "maybe I'd better rephrase that—a good night?"

For once Hannah was glad that her office was small and private. She didn't look forward to justifying her lack of progress to her staff. But Daisy wasn't going to let her get away with silence.

"All right, boss lady, give. What's wrong in fantasyland?"

"I don't know. Everything is wonderful and it's terrible. I can't get anything done. When I'm with him, all I want to do is—"

"Make love? Can't blame you a bit. What about him?"

"The same."

"And that's bad?"

"It's too intense. A person can't spend all the time in bed. Life has to go on. There are other responsibilities. Oh, Daisy, I don't know what to do. I want him so much and yet it's burning me alive."

"Oh, dear. I think we have a problem of degrees here. Of course Ms. Hannah Clendening has never done anything halfway in her life. For almost thirty years you've devoted all your drive and passion toward books and your career. Now something else has stolen that passion, and you don't know how to divide your energy."

"So what do I do? I have to concentrate on my work and *The Morning After.*"

"I don't know about you," Daisy said seriously, "but I'd worry about today and tonight. Tomorrow can take care of itself. That's what you've always done before, and it's worked pretty well."

DON'T HOLD BACK!

1. **No obligation!** No purchase necessary! Enter our Sweepstakes for a chance to win!
2. **FREE!** Get your first shipment of 6 Loveswept books *and* a lighted makeup case as a free gift.
3. **Save money!** Become a member and about once a month you get 6 books for the price of 5! Return any shipment you don't want.
4. **Be the first!** You'll always receive your Loveswept books before they are available in stores. You'll be the first to thrill to these exciting new stories.

Give in to love and see where passion leads you!
Enter the Winners Classic Sweepstakes and
send for your FREE lighted makeup case and
6 FREE Loveswept books today!

(See details inside.)

"You mean work through it like an addict—one hour at a time?"

"Something like that. Maybe you could think about it in terms of rewriting your script."

"How? I've already—I mean, we've—"

"Instead of beginning as friends, you skipped the getting-to-know-you part and fell in love at the start."

"Oh, Daisy. I don't think this is love. It's more like a fatal attraction."

"Then you have to decide whether you want Dan in your life or out of it. You'll survive either way, Hannah. You survived your father's desertion."

Hannah sank down on her chair. "My father? You know he's married again, for the fifth time."

"I heard. I think he has a great deal of courage, or he's a glutton for punishment. It's a good thing he's rolling in money."

"I met his new wife, Gina. She's very different."

"Oh, how?"

"The others were young and beautiful. Gina is— well, motherly, wifely."

"Thank God. There's hope for me."

"She said something very strange. She said I rejected my father."

"And did you?"

"I don't know. I thought it was the other way around. When my mother died, I went to live with her parents in Port Jefferson. C.C. came by from time to time, but I never—I mean it was always awkward. I remember when my grandmother died, he came to the funeral. I was about twelve. Afterward he came to the house and told me to pack my clothes. I was coming with him."

"Why didn't you?"

"I don't know. Port Jefferson was familiar. I had my room and it was where I lived. My grandmother was gone and now this stranger was telling me to leave everything I knew. I said no. My grandfather told my father to leave, and I didn't see him again until I was in college."

"Your grandfather, was he a caring man?"

"I don't know. I suppose. He was a fisherman and gone a lot. He had housekeepers stay with me until I was fifteen. By then I was old enough to stay by myself."

"Sounds lonely."

"No—well, yes, maybe I was. But I had my schoolwork and my books. Then there was boarding school."

"I don't hear you saying much about friends."

"I guess there weren't any close ones, until you came to work with me and refused to stop meddling in my life. But I never noticed."

"So now you've jumped from a life of total fantasy into a red-hot love affair with a man more exciting than any book character, and you don't know how to handle it."

"I suppose you're right."

"Well, Madam Writer, get out your script and your red pencil. I think you need to slow down the relationship. Get to know him before you fall into bed. That's what you'd tell your authors."

Hannah nodded and fell into an uneasy silence. She didn't hear Daisy as she left the office. She was too engrossed in trying to figure out how to quench a flame when it was already blazing. And how to tell a real-life hero that the relationship had to cool down.

Nobody had ever told her that lovemaking was so powerful. And no matter how much she'd read, she'd never seen what she was feeling described on paper.

Hannah didn't know whether she was pleased or displeased when Herb told her that he didn't need the model for Razor Cody anymore. It meant that Dan was free to go whenever he chose. She didn't know how he was doing on his article about prison life, and she hadn't wanted to ask. As long as nothing was settled, she could fool herself into believing that nothing would change.

One part of her was relieved, the other disturbed. Underneath it all, she knew that as long as Dan was in her life, everything had changed, and she wasn't certain that it was for the better.

It was mid-afternoon when Daisy poked her head in Hannah's office. "There's a man on line one about a company car. Said it was in an accident and he's the insurance adjuster. You didn't tell me you had an accident."

Wes Varden. He'd tracked her down as Dan had warned. Or maybe he simply had tracked the car down.

"You didn't tell him I was driving it, did you?"

"Didn't have to," Daisy answered, "he described you to our receptionist perfectly. The only thing he didn't know until he talked to her was your name. Want me to refer him to our lawyer?"

Hannah groaned. "No, I'll talk to him." She laid down the manuscript she'd finally finished editing and picked up the phone. "Yes, this is Hannah Clendening. How may I help you?"

"You can tell me where Bailey is."

"Who?"

"Dan Bailey, the man you picked up at the prison on Saturday."

"Who is this?"

"Wes Varden, *Celebrity* magazine. I was there, Hannah. I saw you and I saw Dan. Either you tell me where he is, or I'll come up with the answers on my own."

"Mr. Varden, I have no idea where Dan Bailey is. And if you want to carry this any further, I suggest you contact our company attorney. C. C. Lowen, the owner, is a very private man and doesn't take kindly to curiosity seekers."

"Fine, but you tell Dan that it's only a matter of time. I already have an idea what he's up to, but I can't figure out where a romance editor fits into the picture. The truth is, it doesn't matter. The picture I took of the two of you kissing in the prison parking lot will be front-page copy."

Eight

Dan didn't answer the phone in the cottage. Hannah left the office early. She had to get home, find him, and tell him about the telephone call. She couldn't get any work done anyway. Thank goodness for Daisy and the progress she'd made in honing her editorial skills. Hannah would do what she should already have done, trust Daisy's judgment and go with her recommendations without insisting on reading every proposal herself.

But Dan wasn't there. He didn't even call. As it grew later and later, Hannah began to worry. She had no right to demand an accounting of his movements. She'd never had a lover before and didn't know the protocol involved. But maybe he didn't consider that they were lovers. They'd made love, yes, over and over, but that didn't make anything official. To Dan it simply might have been sex. She still didn't know why he'd gone to her father's house.

She began to pace. No, it was more than just sex. Even she knew that. Still, the hard cold fact was that if Dan never returned to Port Jefferson, she couldn't force him back into her life.

But she couldn't leave it there. Suppose he'd been hurt somewhere? Suppose someone in the prison got wind of the truth and didn't want Dan to write the article. She'd never heard him say exactly what he was going to write about the inner workings of the prison. Though he hadn't seemed particularly concerned about it, the article might be some dangerous exposé that would cause great repercussions.

Hannah was still dressed in her business suit. She changed into a faded pair of sweats and tennis shoes. Next she made a pot of mint tea, then left the cup half full as she wandered out on the deck and watched the darkness erase the line between the Sound and the sky above it.

Drowned Meadow. Even the name invoked fantasy. Her grandfather had once explained that that's what Port Jefferson had been called in 1664 when the land had been sold to English Puritans. But they'd taken one look at the marshy flat that shifted and changed with the tides and decided their new community would be built west of the meadow.

In the early eighteen hundreds the little village took on the name of the political newspaper, the *Jeffersonian,* and officially called itself Port Jefferson. The house she was living in had been

built about that time and had survived subse-
quent progress only because of her grandfather's
stubborn refusal to get in step with the times.

Hannah thought she must be a lot like the stern
old man she remembered from her childhood. He'd
been a fisherman, and the fact that his daughter
had married a wealthy man hadn't changed his
life. When that daughter died, and her husband
was left with a young child, he and his tyrannical
wife took Hannah in with little comment. When his
own wife had died, her grandfather had seen no
reason to change his lifestyle. His work had taken
him away for long hours on his fishing boat, and
he'd gone. Hannah could manage, he'd believed,
and she had.

Now she had to manage again. Dan had come
into her life, torn apart her protective walls, and
changed her safe, controlled world forever. But
she'd been through upheaval before and survived
without allowing the problems to destroy her.
She'd found a way to cope and she could do it
again.

Still, she couldn't shake the thought that Dan
ought to know what had happened. And she was
back to the fact that she had no idea where he'd
gone, or if he was coming back.

The duffel bag. She took the stairs to the large
bedroom and searched for it. It was still there.

By midnight she'd lost all semblance of any
New England control she might have inherited
from her grandfather. She'd told herself that it
was because she'd been in school in Virginia.
She was having the vapors, like early heroines of

historical romances, whatever vapors were. She'd never known her mother, and she'd lived through the void in her life when her father deserted her. But this was different.

This time she *was* involved, and she had no experience on which to draw. A part of her was gone, given to Dan, and she hadn't replaced it with anything else. Through the waiting hours she allowed herself to admit the truth: she'd fallen in love with Dan Bailey. That had to be, or why would everything inside her hurt so bad? The place where her soul had once existed was now a hollow vacantness.

For the first time in her life she couldn't find answers. There was no forever after, or happy endings—only pain, and she had nowhere to turn.

Gina. She'd go to Gina. Gina would know what to do, and her father would have the means to do it.

Less than an hour later she was ringing the doorbell of the dark house, only half aware of the unexpected stream of wetness across her cheeks.

The door finally opened, and her father, rubbing his eyes, peered out. "Hannah? That you? What's the matter? Come in."

Gina appeared in the hallway behind her father and rushed to Hannah's side. "What's wrong, Hannah?"

"It's Dan."

"Son of a—" her father cursed, and slammed the door. "What has he done to you?"

"Nothing. I mean he—nothing. He's gone. He's vanished, and I'm afraid something bad has happened."

Carl let out an oath and ran his fingers through his hair. "What time is it?"

"It's two o'clock in the morning. Stop swearing, Carl," Gina said sternly. "I'll get Hannah into the den. You wake up Cook and have her make something hot to drink."

To Hannah's surprise, her father complied.

Moments later Hannah was encased in Gina's arms, soaking her robe with tears while her father watched helplessly. Finally Gina pulled back, removed a handful of tissues from her pocket, and began to clean the teardrops from Hannah's face.

"Now, Hannah," Gina said softly, "you've gotten that out of your system. Tell us, what's that scoundrel done?"

"It isn't that. Dan isn't a scoundrel. He hasn't hurt me. He wouldn't do that, and even if he did, it would be for a good reason. It's just that he's missing. I don't know where he is. I mean, it isn't that he has to inform me, but I need to tell him—oh, Gina. I don't know what to do."

"I'll call Captain Dunn," Carl said. "He'll find Dan. Do you know when he left?"

"No, he was in bed when I left for work this morning. I didn't talk to him during the day. Then when that reporter called, I tried to let Dan know that he was about to run our picture."

"Picture? What reporter, Hannah?" Carl pulled up a stool and sat beside his daughter. "Start at the beginning."

"I don't know that I should. Dan told me that his assignment was undercover."

"I don't intend to blow his cover, but I have to know what's going on or I might."

"I picked up Dan when he was being released from Suffolk County Prison."

"Dan was in jail?" Gina shook her head. "I don't believe it. He may be impulsive, but he's not a criminal."

"No, it was set up. He was there to write a story about being in a country club prison. But that's not the problem. Well, it is, but not all of it."

"Go on, dear," Gina encouraged.

"There were reporters at the gate when he was released. They were there to take pictures of some junk-bond king called the Don. One of the photographers, a Wes Varden, works for *Celebrity* magazine. He recognized Dan and he took a picture of us—kissing. He's the problem."

"Wes Varden, I know him," Carl said with a nod. "I'm beginning to see your problem."

At that moment the door opened and the housekeeper, dressed in her nightgown and robe, wheeled a cart in with hot chocolate and pastries. "Will you need anything else, Mrs. Lowenstein?"

Gina shook her head and rose to pour Hannah a cup. "Here, take a sip of this. It will make you feel better."

Hot chocolate, Hannah thought. How many times as a child had she wished for someone to comfort her and offer her chocolate? She'd forgotten that. She'd managed to forget so many things, like the loneliness of her little house, until she had needed Dan and he hadn't been there.

She sipped the chocolate and pushed those thoughts away, concentrating on her father's words. "How do you know Wes Varden, C.C.?"

"He's made a few inquiries about editing the *Ledger*. I turned him down."

"Why?" Hannah emptied her cup. She was surprised. She wouldn't have thought Wes Varden would be interested in editing a small-town newspaper, or that C.C. would hold Wes's experience with the tabloid against him. After all, he couldn't be such a bad reporter, or he wouldn't have been with *World Today*.

"There was some story of his fabricating proof on a story a few years ago. Nothing was ever made public. Wes left the news magazine he was working for, and the matter was dropped. There were some who thought he got off too easy."

"Dan told me there'd been a problem between the two of them too. Wes held Dan responsible for losing his job, didn't he? That's why he's doing this."

Gina refilled Hannah's cup. "What, Hannah? You haven't told us yet what this reporter is doing."

"He's threatened to run a picture of Dan and me. If I don't give him the information he wants about Dan, I'm afraid he'll fabricate his own story."

"Not after I threaten him with a lawsuit, he won't," Carl said.

"No, don't. We can't do anything until we talk to Dan. Oh, C.C.," her voice cracked, "I'm very worried that something has happened to Dan. You see, the picture was taken outside the prison where Dan had been undercover, working on a story. But I don't think the paper knew he was there. He could lose his job—or worse."

"Nobody at *World Today* is going to fire a reporter like Dan Bailey. They may publicly reprimand him, but they'll close their eyes to his methods as long as the facts are right. They know that Dan's a professional; he'll do whatever he has to, to get the story."

"But I don't trust Varden. If he finds out that Dan is the model for our anniversary book cover, he'll make it look—oh, I don't know . . . You see, I promised Dan that nobody would know it was him."

"Why? Are you ashamed of your job, dear?" Gina's question revealed her surprise.

"Not at all. It's Dan I'm worried about. I'm afraid Wes Varden will spoil everything."

"And Dan has disappeared. I'm beginning to wonder what he did learn in that prison." Carl stood and began to saunter back and forth. "I like Dan. I like him even better after having done a little checking on him this morning. Sure, he's stepped on a few toes along the way, and he's cultivated a certain persona of traveling with rich and powerful people to get him where he wants to go. Once I did the same thing."

"You?" Gina lifted her eyebrows in mock disagreement. "I find it hard to believe that you ever pretended to be anything except what you are."

Carl nodded. "There was a time when I did. Of course, I did it out of fear of failure, until I learned that pretending is the worst failure of all. But

Dan's different. The bottom line is that he tells it like it is, and he can't be bought."

"And he doesn't tell you unless he means it," Hannah said softly. "He doesn't pretend."

She wished he did, wished that he'd said he loved her and that he wanted to be with her always. But always was somewhere in the future, and he didn't know that place. All they'd shared was the now. The now was a time she'd learned to live in very well. Until she'd realized that all the hard work in the world wouldn't make a thing permanent if it wasn't meant to be. Until she learned that the romantic descriptions in her novels paled in comparison to falling in love with a real man.

"You're right. We may have a problem," C.C. said. "Let me see what I can do, Hannah."

"You can stay here with us," Gina offered.

"No, I'd better go home. If Dan calls, I ought to be there."

For the first time that she could remember, Hannah hugged her father and meant it. For the first time in her life she felt true emotion when he hugged her back.

But Dan didn't call and he didn't come.

And the next morning, there it was for all the world to see, sensational headlines beyond Hannah's worst nightmare: EX-CON BAD BOY BAILEY AND LATEST LOVER, FANTASY ROMANCE EDITOR HANNAH CLENDENING.

The picture, more revealing than Hannah had thought possible, clearly showed Dan's face and his hand intimately fondling her bottom. He'd pulled her so close that her skirt was hiked up high enough for his fingertips to be resting against the lacy hem of the tap pants she'd been wearing.

"Oh, no!" Hannah groaned. "How could he? That worm!" She scanned the story, which glossed over the why of Dan's sentence, rehashing his recent scrapes over his methods of researching his stories, including his stint as an arms buyer.

From there the story switched to Hannah, the darling of the romance publishing world and her storybook climb to head up a new line called Fantasy Romances. The article went on to suggest that Hannah's research was certainly unique, and made a tongue-in-cheek comment over whether or not there would be a book about their romance.

"Don't kill yourself, boss," Daisy said matter-of-factly. "This only means that you've joined the ranks of the rich and famous. Look what happens to them every issue. If there's no news, these guys manufacture it."

"Daisy, when you told me to write my own script, I never expected anything like this. What do you suppose our readers will say?"

"My guess is that if they find out that you and Dan were the models for *The Morning After*, it will make *The New York Times* best-seller list."

"They'd better not. Don't you dare tell them. Fantasy makes it on the basis of the books or not at all."

"Uh-huh, if you think that's always the way it works, I have a bridge over in Brooklyn I'd like to sell you. Chin up, it was simply an accident that your picture was taken. Or maybe it was fate, and we don't yet know why it was destined to happen."

"I can't believe that. And where is Dan?"

"Now there's a question you can worry about. You haven't seen him since that creep called?"

"Nope. He hasn't been home and he hasn't called. C.C. is making some quiet inquiries, but nobody seems to know, including his friend Pete and his editor. He's supposed to be on vacation."

"Dan? On vacation? That's about as likely as you taking one. Besides, this will blow over in a heartbeat. By tomorrow there will be some new scandal to take the public's mind off this. I hate to say it, Hannah, but this isn't the juiciest story since Madonna's steel-plated bra."

Daisy was wrong. The next morning brought inquiries from two different tabloid television programs and a note from Oprah sympathizing with the invasion of Hannah's privacy and asking if she might consider appearing on a program about country-club-prison wives and lovers.

"That's it," Hannah announced, slinging manuscripts and proposals into her briefcase. "I'm going home. Daisy, you've been promoted to editor. Edit!"

The train to Port Jeff was leaving as she got to the station. During the hour-and-a-half ride, she forced herself to read the first proposal she pulled from her briefcase. By the time she reached her stop, she'd decided that the author was simply too cute and her attempts at humor only made the heroine look silly. She'd read it again. It wasn't fair to make her decision when she was remembering her own romance and the anguish that had overwhelmed her since Dan disappeared.

She stopped first at the local market, then took a cab to her house. The driver carried her bags to the door, then left. As Hannah unlocked the door she heard voices inside. "Dan?"

She opened the door and dropped her briefcase and the bag she was carrying on the counter. The stereo was playing. The computer was on, and the door to the deck was open.

Dan was outside, standing on the far corner of the deck, staring at the ocean as if he were carrying the weight of the world on his shoulders.

"Dan, where have you been?"

"Thinking."

"Are you all right?"

He turned to face her, all the pain he'd stored up visible in his eyes. "No. I don't suppose I am. But then, I don't suppose I was ever meant to be. I'm only sorry that I got you involved in my life."

"You're wrong. I think it was me who got you involved in mine. Have you seen *Celebrity* magazine?"

"Yes."

"What are you going to do?"

"I'm going to turn in my story and then—I don't know. Head for some new place, some new town where people don't know Dan Bailey."

"Your job?"

"You mean the job I used to have? Gone. I quit."

"Over the story about the prison corruption?"

"No, that isn't what I wrote, Hannah. My story was about the Don and his political connections.

But it's my disgust and disillusionment with the business I'm a part of that has gotten to me."

"I see."

But she didn't. She didn't understand what all this meant. *What about me?* Hannah folded one arm across her body, holding the other. She felt as if she were rooted to the floor, as though every ounce of her life's blood were running out and soaking into the dry, dead wood flooring on which she was standing.

"Oh, Dan, I'm so sorry. Poor Razor didn't know what he was letting himself in for when he joined up with Miss Rachel Kimbel. He didn't get his revenge after all."

"I think maybe he did. I'd say it was poor Rachel. She got caught up in Razor's past and was singed by his fire."

"And she loved every minute of it."

He simply said, "Hannah, I'm sorry. I let myself want you, and I shouldn't have."

"But I want—wanted you too."

And then he was holding her. They made their way into the house and up the stairs, shedding their clothes, kissing, touching.

He captured her mouth and held it with desperation, his hands kneading her body, his breath coming fast and uneven. They fell across the bed, reaching for each other, using their bodies to say things their rational minds refused to admit.

"I don't care what happened," she said over and over. "Nothing matters but us and this."

"I want you, angel, here and now. You're all I've ever wanted."

The need to claim and brand and commit to memory bordered on desperation as the cloud of heat that had followed them from the first ignited and consumed them with fire.

Dan felt his primitive instincts rise up, the strength he'd intended to maintain evaporating in his desire. He pinned her to the bed, then clasped her in his arms, moving against her, searing her skin with his essence.

At last he entered her, and she caught the headboard behind her, holding on, painfully biting her lip to keep Dan from knowing how perilously close she was to crying out that she loved him. Instead she thrust against him, giving, saying with her body what words didn't dare. And then it happened, the breath-stopping release that propelled them past here and now. They were flying, reaching the farthest limits of exaltation.

"You know I have to go," he said at last.

"Don't."

"I must."

"I know."

"I've never wanted to stay before."

"I've never wanted anybody to stay."

"Will this story harm you as an editor?"

"It doesn't matter. Once I thought I *was* my books. I'm not. They will stand alone, as will I."

He squeezed her shoulder and planted a kiss on her forehead. "I wish I could change it."

"No. I wouldn't change a thing."

"When will Razor's book be out?"

"It's a January release, out in December. I'll send you a copy. The cover turned out pretty fantastic."

"I'd better pick one up. I don't know where I'll be."

What Dan was saying was that he wouldn't be with her. Hannah didn't answer. She didn't know what to say.

They made love again, slowly, quietly, with a certain poignancy that said they understood that their time had come to an end, understood and accepted.

When Hannah awoke the next morning, Dan was gone. His duffel bag was no longer in her closet, and his document had been erased from her computer. As she stood in the middle of her little house it was as if he'd never been there.

She sat on the deck drinking her coffee and thought about her books and her authors. In a novel, she wouldn't have let Dan leave without talking. Her authors knew that modern women didn't retreat into their past and let things happen. Every heroine was master of her own fate—except her. She should have asked Dan why he was leaving, where he was going, and told him she wanted him to stay.

But it didn't work like that in real life, at least not in hers. She'd fallen in love with a man who wanted to make love to her, but didn't love her. And now he was gone.

The house was lonely and quiet, as it had been when she was a child. Except she wasn't a child anymore. She hadn't written her own script very well. Hannah knew that she'd survive, but her little cottage would never be so alive again.

And neither would she.

Nine

Herb made Hannah a present of the painting of Rachel and Razor.

Hannah took the mirror down and hung the painting over the mantel. They hadn't needed to use the photograph, the artist had captured the aura of their desire on canvas. After spending one entire afternoon staring at the painting, Hannah had to stop looking at it, it was too intense, too painful.

The painting was all she had of Dan. She couldn't look, but she couldn't bear to take it down.

The June issue of *World Today* ran a short story on the second page, under Dan's byline, exposing Suffolk County Prison's recent famous inmate, the junk-bond king, called the Don, as a member of the once powerful Cascillio family. The family had a history of using their investment and banking businesses in three countries to launder their drug income. Dan's exposé of the prisoner was the final chapter in the Cascillio family's dirty-money dealings.

Hannah understood now why Dan had been in the prison. The next week she received a short note from Dan, saying that he was going to try to get his life in order. Hannah wished him more luck than she was having. Since Dan disappeared, she hadn't been able to reclaim that peaceful solitude she'd always enjoyed. She found herself spending more and more time with her father and Gina.

In May she attended a book lovers' conference in San Diego where her authors were the center of attention. The booksellers in the audience of her workshop had learned about her special attention to the book covers, even recognizing her on the display copy of *The Morning After*. When one of the keen-eyed fans asked about the latest article in *Celebrity* that charged Hannah had been dumped, Hannah admitted that the relationship was over. All true romantics at heart, the conference attendees didn't have to be told how the book characters, Razor and Rachel, felt about each other; the painter had captured it all. Those closest to Hannah knew the truth; the aura in the painting belonged to Hannah and Dan.

Long before she got the doctor's report, Hannah knew. She thought about finding Dan and telling him, then decided not to. Instead she began turning the room she had lived in as a girl into a nursery.

It had happened that last day, when they'd been so overcome with emotion and regret that neither had considered the consequences.

Now she was going to have a child, Dan's child. And though she'd never been one of those women who worried about their biological clock, she was delighted.

"Falling in love is the promise, Daisy. Having a child is keeping it."

"Maybe," Daisy answered, "but in my day it was called paying the piper. Of course, I can't remember a piper who looked like Razor Cody, or I might have been willing to pay. Count on me as chief babysitter."

"I'm hiring a new secretary and promoting Bets to be your assistant, Daisy. I want you to start training her."

"And what is the boss going to do, go home and pregnate?"

"Of course not. I'm still going to work, I just have to make room in my life for something other than Fantasy Romances."

"Have you made any attempt to locate Dan, Hannah?"

"No, and I'm not going to. This is my child, and I'll raise it myself."

"Uh-huh, like your grandfather raised you."

"I think I turned out all right," Hannah snapped, knowing what Daisy was saying gave voice to her most secret doubts. Gina had given her much the same talking-to when she'd learned of Hannah's pregnancy. C.C. had blustered that he'd find the boy and bring him back.

But Hannah refused to allow him to look.

Dan had never made her any promises, and she wouldn't ask anything of him. Falling in love with Dan didn't give her any right to tie him down. She suspected that Dan's photographer knew where he was, and if she'd wanted Dan to know about her condition, she'd have sent him a message.

She was doing fine, tough upper lip and all that, until Christmas drew near. She was still working, but not as hard. She was no longer driven. She was still wearing her power suits and business pumps, but she found herself slowing down, through choice, not because she wasn't feeling well. In fact she'd never felt better physically. Emotionally, behind closed doors and in the middle of the night, she walked the floor and turned to reading mysteries and science fiction.

It became harder and harder to read about living happily ever after. And there was no way that mere words could express the loneliness or the pain. She'd never read a romance where the hero and heroine blazed so hot that they burned themselves up in the fire of their passion.

Port Jefferson's annual lighting of the Christmas tree came and went. Hannah hadn't put up a tree. She hadn't done that for the last few years. She'd never formed any Christmas traditions, and she'd told herself that she hadn't missed the warmth of family and friends.

Until this year, when the lie loomed before her every time she walked past the bedroom and stood over the crib in the nursery.

Dan put down the correspondence he was trying to answer. It was no use, he couldn't concentrate. He'd thought that returning to Augusta was the right thing to do. He couldn't straighten out his present life until he'd righted the old wrongs. He'd turned his back on his father and brother years ago because he'd thought they were joining the "good old boy" network from tradition, not because they truly wanted to help the people they dealt with. For years, he'd fought the restraints of being a Bailey, of living up to his father's expectations, of following the example set by his brother.

But he'd been wrong. His father *was* a good old boy, but he was a good judge too, tempering punishment with mercy and working with Dan's brother in making laws to correct injustice. Managing his brother's office was a full-time job, and his family was pleased with his return.

He tried to force himself to fit in. He'd cut his hair and removed his earring. He turned away the calls Pete forwarded to him from rival publications, newspapers, even a couple of television stations. For most of his life he'd gone where the wind blew him, followed the sun and raced the moon. But suddenly there was nowhere he wanted to go and nothing he wanted to do. Except see Hannah again.

But seeing Hannah again would be making a promise, a promise he wasn't certain he could keep.

Beautiful Hannah—caught up in the magic of her world, striving to achieve the impossible dream, watching falling stars and wishing for forever. Being with her had been the single most intense time of his life. He'd met with kings and heads of state, but he'd never been as captivated by anyone as he had with Hannah.

He'd made love to women he'd liked and a few he'd genuinely cared for, but nothing had happened to rock him the way loving Hannah had. Even the thought of her made his pulse quicken. But he'd brought the ugliness of his life into the fantasy of hers. And he'd hurt her.

Dan had offered Wes the real story of the identity of the Don in return for keeping the story about Hannah off the front page. But exposing the Don as being part of the Cascillio family wouldn't sell as many rag sheets as the gossip about Hannah and Dan. So the tabloid ran their picture instead.

Once scum, always scum.

Dan went after Wes and found him in a bar. Only because the judge who arranged his time in the prison was the same one he came before when Wes swore out a warrant for assault, did he escape serving more time in jail. Wes had a broken tooth and Dan a fractured rib. The judge took them into chambers and strongly suggested that both men get their acts together. When they concurred, he dismissed the charges.

For the first time since he'd left home, Dan had no assignment. So he gave himself one. *Go home to Georgia and do what the judge said, "get your life together."* Now he got up every morning, went down to his brother's office to work. His plan to freelance never quite materialized, nor did the fleeting thought he had of writing a book. He was a journalist. At least he had been; now he wasn't certain what he was.

All of that seemed so unimportant.

And then his mother put up the Christmas tree, cajoling him to help her string the lights.

"What are you doing, Danny?" she'd asked that night in the den.

"Doing? Trying to untangle this strand of lights, Mother."

"No, I mean here, in Augusta. You're my child and I love you, but you don't belong here anymore. Who is she?"

He plugged the strand in and was rewarded when the lights all burned. "She?"

"The woman who's turned you inside out. Is she the woman in that magazine?"

"You saw it?"

"I did. I was the most infamous woman in the beauty shop for three weeks running, then Sophie Murphy tore the front cover off and took it home. She probably stuck it on her refrigerator so she could drool over you every time she reaches for another ice cream bar.

"Mother!"

"I can't wait to meet her. She'll look lovely in your sister-in-law's wedding gown."

"Mother, Hannah is six inches taller than Isabella. Besides, there isn't going to be a wedding. We hardly know each other."

"Well, I'd say that's your fault. From the look of that picture you certainly said a powerful hello."

Dan stood and wound the strand of lights around the tree, then unfastened another one, holding it and thinking. His mother was right. They had said a powerful hello, and from that point on they'd been engulfed in a maelstrom of pure desire. It had come at him from all sides, so powerfully that he hadn't been able to see or feel anything, except desire for Hannah.

But it had been more than that. He'd felt good, normal even, being with her. They hadn't talked much, but they'd been able to tell each other things that they hadn't told anyone else. For the first time, he'd realized that he didn't know where he was going. Like Hannah, he'd turned away from a family that he had nothing in common with and found a place where he belonged. Except he didn't belong anymore. Before he'd come home, he'd tried moving back in with Pete, hanging out at the old places, meeting with other writers and exchanging stories as he always had.

But it was different. His friends listened for a while, then started in on their I-can-top-that stories, often interrupting before he'd finished the point of his tale. He began to feel as if he were in some kind of bragging contest, little boys bragging that "my daddy can beat your daddy."

When had it changed? When had he started wishing that Hannah could share something, see something, tell him what she thought about something? When had Hannah's reaction become more important than his own?

Was it that way for others? He thought about Carl Lowenstein and his easy relationship with his new wife, Gina. Even Hannah had admitted in disbelief that Gina was nothing like the other women his father had married. She'd softened Carl, turning him into a different man. Gina was a wife, a companion, a friend.

Hannah would be like that.

"Dan!" his mother interrupted. "Hand me those lights. I want to get this tree up for this Christmas, not next."

"Next?" he repeated absently as he began to string the lights.

"Next Christmas. Of course, by that time I'm thinking you'll be somewhere in your own home. And who knows? I might even be a grandmother again."

"Grandmother?" That thought took his breath away.

"You do intend to get married someday, don't you?"

"I—I hadn't thought that I would." As for his producing grandchildren for his mother, it was unlikely to happen. He'd been very careful to protect Hannah. He knew how ambitious she was, how important her fast-paced lifestyle was to her. The last thing she'd need in her life was a baby.

His baby. He'd never felt particularly fatherly before. Families belonged to other people who stayed in one place. He never had time for that.

And that, in a nutshell, was part of the problem; staying in one place. He'd lost his killer instinct. Now he was going crazy staying in his own home in his own hometown. Hannah was settled where she was. Home and place were important to her, as was her career. Being editor-in-chief of a successful publishing company wasn't something you could do between flights, or in some foreign country where electricity was paid for with coins and was only available for a few hours each day.

Hannah couldn't bear to leave her place in time, and Dan couldn't wait to leave his. But to go where? What happened when a man had no place left he wanted to go?

"When does that book come out, anyway?" Mrs. Bailey asked. "I'm looking forward to reading it."

The book. Dan had forgotten about the book. Razor's book. His book. His mother didn't seem surprised when he found a sudden errand he had to run.

The mall was crowded with Christmas shoppers. A long line of people shimmied around the courtyard where Santa Claus had moved into Wonderland.

Standing at the back of the line was a mother and a little girl, a little girl with taffy-colored hair. She was wearing a pink coat, the same color as the dress Hannah had worn the night they'd had dinner with her father. Looking up at Santa with wide eyes filled with excitement, Dan felt a sudden rush of emotion.

The woman could be Hannah. Alone, with her child. Where was the father? How could he bear to miss such a special time with his family?

Dan watched for a long time before realizing that he was allowing himself to wallow in self-pity. He didn't have a family. Families didn't fit into the life of a world traveler, even when he'd stopped to restructure his life. Dan hurried past the end of the line and headed for the bookstore.

The store owner turned out to be an old high school friend who offered to help if Dan needed assistance.

Dan didn't. He wandered casually down the aisle, picking up a book, glancing at it, then replacing it on the rack. He needn't have worried about finding Razor's book—it filled an entire section, practically leaping off the shelf at him. There were two women standing there, discussing the cover.

"I heard about this book, Ann. Read in one of the romance magazines that it was rated a four-plus and won the Fantasy Lover award."

"Yeah, well, I'd buy it if it got a zero-minus. Will you look at those two. The paper is even hot when I touch it."

The first reader gave her friend a frown of disapproval. "That's all you're interested in, how hot a romance is. Personally, I'm more concerned about the characters and the relationship."

"You read it for the characters, I'll read it for the romance. Seriously, Pat, the book's got both. I've heard it's dynamite."

Dan waited until they left the section and picked up a copy of the book. For a moment he would have sworn that the second reader was right. The paper was hot to the touch, then he realized that it was him. Looking at the cover put him right back on Hannah's deck.

Right back in Hannah's arms.

Loving Hannah.

He tucked his copy of *The Morning After* between two other books and went to the cashier's desk, hoping that the clerk would simply take his money without comment. He wasn't that lucky.

"Hey, Dan," his friend called, "that's an interesting selection you have there: a book on shipbuilding, one on modern relationships, and a romance novel?"

"My mother asked me to pick up the romance."

"Hmm. I wouldn't want it to get out," the manager confided, "but I enjoy reading that romance line myself. It's kinda addictive."

"You don't know the half of it."

"And those two on the cover—Wow! The guy looks familiar, doesn't he?"

Dan paid for his books and hurried from the shop before the manager made the connection between the model and Dan.

All the way home Dan thought about the woman on the cover of the book, about Hannah. He'd refused to recognize what he saw in her eyes, preferring to think of their affair as intense and short. But there was no hiding from the truth any longer. It was there, on the book cover, open and honest. The two people on the book cover were in love.

There was no more pretending.

He and Hannah had fallen in love. He hadn't given Hannah a chance. He'd left her. He'd become the thing he'd sworn not to: a promise not kept.

Unless—

An early snowfall peppered the air on Saturday afternoon. Hannah went out for a walk, feeling the buffeting winds at her back pushing her up the hill. She unlocked her door and closed it against the wind with a slam.

Daisy hadn't come up for the weekend. Her family in Brooklyn had some kind of Christmas feast planned. C.C. had called and offered to send a car for Hannah to join him and Gina for dinner, but she'd begged off. She felt clumsy and fat. Nothing seemed right about the day. From the time she'd awakened, there'd been an electricity in the air, a kind of waiting that intensified with every hour.

It was the middle of December, and the baby wasn't due for another month. It couldn't be that. The doctor had done all the tests and said everything was fine. He'd offered to tell her whether her baby was a boy or a girl. She refused. All she wanted to hear were the words "The baby's fine."

It was her life that was all wrong. Dan ought to be with her. Hannah changed into a flannel nightgown and a warm robe. She lit the fire in the fireplace, but there was no warmth.

The sky grew darker, the wind rose. From the deck she watched the gray water roll in toward the harbor and crash against the stone wall. The sailboats and pleasure craft anchored in the Sound bobbled precariously, slamming against their slots as if they were angry at being restrained.

She could see the village Christmas tree swaying in the breeze, the flickering lights strung along the street. Inside the row of restored eighteenth-century houses, brightly lit trees twinkled merrily. Next year she'd put up a tree—for the baby. Her baby would have memories, even without a father.

She allowed herself a big dose of self-pity. She felt like crying; the tears hovered there, just behind her eyelids, caught in the painful tightening of her throat.

There was a knock on her door.

Ten

"Dan? Is it really you?"

"In the flesh, Miss Rachel," Dan said in his best Humphrey Bogart imitation. "Dan Bailey, also known as the infamous Razor Cody."

Hannah couldn't believe it. He took her breath away, just as he had that day at the prison. All she could say was, "You're wearing a trenchcoat!"

"Yes. There's a storm brewing. May I come in?"

"Yes." Hannah stepped back and watched the man she'd dreamed about nightly for months walk through her door. "I'm surprised to see you."

"It feels good to be here."

Dan had thought to take her in his arms and mount the stairs, to take off her clothes and make slow, beautiful love to the woman who'd haunted him for months. But her blue eyes were staring at him as if he were a stranger, a stranger she was afraid of.

Hannah couldn't seem to move. Hadn't he noticed? She'd been lucky. Even though she felt huge, she carried her pregnancy well, and the robe she was wearing was big and flowing. She stood by the door and watched Dan. In her dreams he'd taken her in his arms and smothered her with kisses. But he wasn't doing that. His eyes were filled with wariness, almost as if he knew and he were daring her to say something.

"You've cut your hair, Dan," she said softly, talking about inconsequential things instead of the larger truth that had made her speechless.

"Does that mean I'm no longer a gorgeous tattooed, dirt-breathing man of the earth?"

You're still gorgeous, and you were never a dirt-breathing man of the earth, she whispered under her breath, "Your earring is gone. You look quite—sophisticated. Do you still have your tattoo?"

"Yes. I'm still the same."

But he wasn't. The brash, roguish Dan who'd been her lover was gone. He'd been a fantasy, her fantasy come to life. This man was a stranger. "The same," she whispered, "only different."

"So are you. There's something about you . . . I can't quite put my finger on it, but there's something very different." She was holding the ties of her robe, her arms crossed beneath her breasts. It was almost as if she were holding her breath.

"Why did you come, Dan?"

"I saw our book. I saw us. I had to."

"Did you like it?"

"It was overwhelming." It had hit him in the stomach with something akin to a missile exploding and sending fire through his body. Fire that he hadn't been able to control or extinguish.

"The painting is even more spectacular than the book cover." She lifted her eyes, casting her gaze to the fireplace.

He followed her vision and let out a sharp sigh. The painting was magnificent. She was right. It was even more powerful than the cover. Powerful and poignant. There they were, the reckless, devil-may-care Razor Cody and the feisty, determined Miss Rachel Kimbel. They weren't just two models, they were real. There was a cloud of heat around them that transcended the canvas.

"Where did all that heat come from?" he murmured.

"Where did it go?"

"I don't believe that it has. We've just damped the fire, it isn't gone. It can't be. Hannah, we shared more than a week. We changed each other's lives."

Hannah gave a dry laugh. "At the risk of sounding completely corny, I have to say 'you can say that again.' Take off your coat, Dan."

Dan slid his arms out of the trench coat and hung it on the brass coatrack by the door. He looked back to find Hannah still standing in the same spot. The firelight flickered on her hair like sunlight on fine gold jewelry.

"You let your hair grow out."

"Yes. I pin it up now." It's easier, she started to say, then changed it to, "It makes me look more professional."

They were talking, yet the words were empty. Hannah had a stricken look about her, as if she were going to be reprimanded and was waiting for it to begin. He'd never felt so unsure in his life.

"What's happened, Hannah? Why are we behaving like strangers?"

"Maybe we are."

"I thought we were friends."

"I don't think we were ever friends."

"No," he agreed. "We were more."

She moistened her lips, catching the lower one briefly between her teeth. "Lovers, but we never knew each other."

"I didn't think we had to. We knew ourselves and we were reflections of the other."

"Perhaps, but you're a man and I'm a woman, and sometimes we don't look at things the same. Even if we did, things change."

It had to be done. She couldn't conceal her pregnancy from Dan. If they hadn't been so caught up in the emotional awakening of their reunion, he'd have noticed. She might as well get it over with. "Have a seat and get ready for a shock." Hannah let go the ties of her robe and walked toward the fire, deliberately placing her profile between Dan and the flames.

"Hannah. You're pregnant!"

"Yes. I seem to be."

"You're very pregnant!"

"Very pregnant. In fact I think I'm the one who'd better sit down. This has been a bit of a shock, seeing you here."

Dan shook off the paralyzing state of recognition and rushed to Hannah's side. He reached out helplessly, taking her hand and then releasing it as she caught the arm of the couch and sat.

"Do I need to do something, call a doctor?"

Hannah laughed lightly. "Dan Bailey, you've done quite enough. Come and sit down and I'll tell you what you haven't asked."

Dan first sat in the chair beside the sofa, then got up and sat uneasily beside Hannah. "I don't know what to ask."

"You want to know if this baby is yours. Well, it isn't. It's mine. You want to know if I intend to ask you for anything. I don't. I'm managing fine."

It wasn't her saying that the baby was hers that got to him, it was her saying that she was managing fine. He could look at the uncertainty in her eyes and see that she wasn't fine. Instead of Hannah's confident spirit, he saw the lonely, abandoned little girl who read about life in books and fantasized about the heroes inside them.

That was when he got mad. The last time he'd gotten mad, Wes Varden had suffered a broken tooth and Dan had gone before the judge. This time he simply stood up and, towering over Hannah, began to count.

"One—two—" Anything to hold on to his anger.

"I think the next line is 'buckle my shoe.' But I'm not wearing any."

He glanced down. She wasn't. The toes on her bare feet peeked out from the hem of her robe.

"Where are your house shoes, Hannah?" he roared. "You'll catch a cold, and that isn't good for our baby. I'll get them."

He dashed up the stairs, caught sight of the open door to Hannah's old room, and glanced in. Gone was the yesterday look Hannah had frozen in time. Now the room was a whimsical, magical place. The walls had been adorned with blooming flowers, smiling animals, waterfalls, and boats. Safely away from the window was a crib that looked like a brass-railed chest, all shiny and new. Overhead a carousel of brass bells and fairy creatures moved with the air.

The room was warm and wonderful. Every accoutrement spoke of love and joy. Dan felt a pain somewhere beneath his breastbone. Hannah had done this, for their child, alone.

He turned and moved slowly back down the stairs.

"Why, Hannah? Why didn't you get in touch with me?"

"Where?"

"Your father could have found me."

"Why? If you'd wanted me to know, you would have told me yourself."

"But there's the baby, Hannah. Not just you."

"If I didn't matter, why would my child?"

"Our child, dammit! Our child. You're having our child."

"Yes, I am." She leaned her head back against the couch. There was her familiar shortness of breath and a dull ache in her lower back. She let out a deep breath, then another.

"What's wrong? Tell me, what's wrong, Hannah?"

"Wrong? My feet are too swollen to get into my shoes. I look like a pear with arms and legs, and my back aches. Now the man I've wished would appear for eight months is looking at me as if he hates all fruit, and pears in particular."

Dan dropped to his knees beside the couch and took one of Hannah's feet in his hands. "They're cold. Let me warm them." He moved to sit beside her once more, lifting her feet and turning her so that her legs lay across his lap.

Hannah's feet were cold, but Dan's hands weren't. Almost instantly she felt a tingle of warmth. He began to massage, sliding his fingertips across her instep, around her heel and back, then moving to the toes, where he paid attention to each one individually. Once he was satisfied with one foot, he turned to the other, watching her as he worked.

She was still the most beautiful woman he'd ever known. Her creamy skin took on the delicate color of some porcelain sculpture in the firelight. Her slender neck was long and lovely. Her breasts were larger. He could see the way they strained against her gown and robe. But the part of her that most captured his attention was her softly rounded stomach.

All the way from Georgia to Long Island he'd planned this meeting, planned how he'd take her in his arms and make wonderful love to her. Now he was loving her in a very different way, and deep inside he felt a glow of satisfaction that was new.

His hands moved upward, cupping her knees, moving rhythmically across her thighs to touch her there, where she carried their child. Hannah's breathing quickened for a moment, and her eyes opened.

"Don't do this, Dan. I survived your leaving me once; I don't want to have to do it again."

"It's still there, Hannah, the heat."

"No, it's only the aftermath, the memory. You're familiar, and I'm vulnerable right now. The desire may still be there, but that's all."

She struggled to sit, pulling herself upright, the movement catching her robe beneath her, pulling it open.

Dan didn't know what he'd expected, but after seeing the silky teddy she once slept in, he wasn't expecting a flannel nightgown. He smiled.

"Very chic," he said. "Not as exciting as the teddy, but I've been told that motherhood kills the sex drive. That's all right, for now. We'll worry about rekindling it later."

"Don't talk like that, Dan." *Don't make me remember or think about the future. Let's concentrate on the now. I'll get through it the way I did your leaving, one day at a time.*

"All right. I'll wait. Have you eaten?"

"No. No, I haven't. I haven't been very hungry today."

"Let me bring my bag inside out of the storm, and I'll see what I can stir up in the kitchen."

"Your bag?"

He'd headed toward the front door, opened it, and reached down for the bag he'd left outside. "Of course. You don't think that I'm letting you stay here alone?"

"But I've been alone for most of my life."

"Not anymore."

Hannah lumbered to her feet. "Now just a minute, Dan Bailey. Just because I'm having your baby doesn't give you the right to move in and try to take over my life."

"Oh, I'm not. I'm going to share it with you. I'll even pay rent, once I get a job. What about child care? What arrangements have you made for our baby when you're ready to go back to work?"

"I'm going to work at home for a while. I'll only go in two days a week. I'm still interviewing nannies."

"That sounds reasonable. And I'm glad to hear you admit that it's *our* baby. Of course, I'll fill in too."

"You, a nanny?"

"You told me once I could be a model, and I was a good one. I can be as good as a nanny. Now, about those cold feet, I think I know just the thing. Wait here."

He disappeared up the stairs, whistling a merry chorus of "Jingle Bells." Seconds later he'd changed into a red pullover sweater and returned, holding a pair of bright green socks in his hands.

"Sit over here on one of these stools."

"Wishful thinking," Hannah said. "I can't get on a stool, it's too high, and I can't get up from a chair that's too low."

"Fine, I'll lift you." Effortlessly he picked Hannah up and placed her on the stool. Almost automatically her hand reached out and touched his cheek, feeling the instant flare of heat between them, heat and hope. She let out a deep sigh and turned her head, swallowing desperately to release the tightness in her throat. No, she wasn't going to let this happen, not now, not again.

For a long, intense moment Dan stayed where he was, then he let her go and knelt before the stool, uncovering her feet from beneath her robe. His green socks fit her feet perfectly, and she immediately felt the return of the warmth that had vanished when Dan left her side.

"Is that better?"

"Yes."

"Forgive me, Hannah."

"I forgive you, Dan. I really do. I understood that it all happened too quickly. It was too intense. It couldn't have lasted."

"Yes, if I'd been willing to deal with—with us instead of running off like some scared fool."

"No, Dan. Don't. This isn't going to work."

"Why do you say that?" He moved around the counter and opened the refrigerator. "I'll find a job. I don't intend to live off my—your income. There's still a newspaper or two that will take a chance on me."

"I know that, Dan. It's us, being here together. It isn't going to work. You said it before. We're much too potent together; we burn each other up."

"Ah, but you know what happens after a fire. The banked coals continue to glow. All you have to do to keep it going is feed it occasionally. And that is what I'm about to do, feed you."

Hannah pressed her hand against the small of her back and tried to ignore the pain that seemed to be increasing. It had to be the emotional impact of seeing Dan. She'd felt his coming all day; her unease and discomfort had increased along with the forewarnings of the storm.

Suddenly she couldn't be still any longer. She caught the edge of the counter and managed to slide awkwardly to the floor, her stockinged feet padding soundlessly toward the glass door overlooking the water. Movement, that seemed to help.

"What about an omelet? I'm an omelet chef extraordinaire."

"Really, Dan," she said breathlessly, "I don't think I can eat anything."

Then it hit, a sharp pain, racking her back where the dull ache had only nagged. "Ahhhh!"

Dan jerked his head up, colliding with the freezer section of the refrigerator with a resounding whack. "Damn!" He backed out, rubbing his head. Hannah was leaning against the door. "What's wrong?"

"I'm not sure, Dan Bailey, but I'm afraid this child is as out of control as you."

"You don't mean it's coming now?"

"Not instantly, but soon."

"Oh hell! What should we do?"

"There's not much you can do. This is one job that I have to handle myself." She gasped and straightened up. "It's passed for the moment."

"What happens now?"

"We wait."

"But is that safe?"

"That's the way it happens, Dan. Cook your omelet. It may be hours, and then again it might be a false alarm."

"You think I can eat at a time like this?"

"I don't know why not, you're not in labor."

The wind whistled, blowing a fresh peppering of icy snow against the glass door and rattling it ominously. Hannah walked slowly back toward the couch and the fire. She wasn't cold anymore, and she couldn't get Dan's description of feeding the banked coals out of her mind.

Just a simple touch had flared the heat between them. What was wrong with her? Here she was more than eight months pregnant, in labor for heaven's sake, and she was craving his touch. It wasn't supposed to be like this. She'd gotten over him, written him out of her manuscript.

The phone rang, shattering the awkward silence.

"I'll get it, Hannah. Just be still, or move around, or do whatever feels good."

Hannah groaned.

"Hello?"

"Either I've reached the wrong number, or God has answered my prayers. Is this the hunk of the month?"

"Daisy? How come you aren't here? Hannah's in labor, and I don't know what to do."

"The two of you figured out how to make a baby, you'll figure out how to get it here."

"Daisy, this is not funny. This is serious. I don't need some wisecracking, smart-aleck answer. We need you, Daisy."

"No, Dan, what you need is a doctor. His number is right beside the phone. Give him a call."

Behind him Dan heard Hannah groan again. This time she doubled up in pain. Dan hung up the phone and hurried to her side, helping her to sit down.

"I'm calling the doctor, Hannah, no matter what you say."

"Fine, call him."

Dan hurried back to the phone, located the number, and dialed. He got the answering service, who took the message and number.

Before Dan could get back to Hannah, the phone rang again. "Hello, Dr. Cross, she's having our baby."

"This isn't Dr. Cross," Gina's voice said with a laugh. "Is this Dan?"

"Of course, I'm the father. Who else did you expect?"

"Just like a journalist. Get there at the last minute, in time to make your deadline. Let us know what happens."

"But you don't understand. I don't know what to do."

"You hold her hand and rub her back, and she'll do the rest."

"Rub her back? But that's not the part that's pregnant."

Gina chuckled. "Restrain yourself, Dan. That's the part that's hurting. No point in setting up conflicting situations. Keep the hands where the hurt is."

"Dan, my water just broke. Hang up the phone."

"Water?" Dan simply stared at the dark puddle of wetness and felt his heart drop. "Hannah, what should I do?"

"Dan, get me upstairs so that I can clean up."

"Yes, of course."

He felt her contraction as he carried her up the stairs and into the bathroom. Quickly he found a fresh gown and robe and helped her change. He knew what he was thinking was clichéd, but he couldn't improve on it. Seeing her beautiful body swollen with his child was the most profound experience of his life.

Carrying her to the car proved a bit tricky, but they managed. Halfway to the hospital he remembered her bag, in the hallway, by the door.

"Doesn't matter," Hannah said. "I won't need any of that stuff right away anyway." She groaned and caught his leg, pinching it painfully as she began to breathe in short, shallow pants.

"Hannah, what's wrong?"

"Nothing, Dan. This is what I'm supposed to do. Drive. The hospital is straight up—"

"I know where it is. I can see the sign."

Moments later they were in a labor room. Half an hour later Gina and Carl joined them. Joe had to pick up Daisy at the station, so it took them longer to arrive.

On the way to her delivery room, Hannah had sworn not to succumb to Dan's charm, not depend on him, not to let herself make him a part of her baby's birth. And yet she couldn't let go of his hand.

Giving birth was harder than she'd expected. The pain was worse, and the need to touch and share was greater than she'd ever dreamed. And Dan was there, with his smoky eyes filled with concern and uncertainty. His huge hand alternately held her and rubbed her back. When he strayed a bit off course now and then, she tried to ignore it.

Between pains she faced the truth. A woman in labor could feel desire, no matter how much pain she was racked with, and no matter that the room was turning into a three-ring circus. What did that make her?

Helpless and shameless and in love.

"Dan," she whispered. "I don't want you to see me like this. I'm so ugly."

"You think I'm leaving now? I'll get ugly too. What can I do?"

"There's not a way in heaven that you could ever be ugly, Dan," she said.

"And neither are you."

Dan leaned down and kissed her forehead, her cheeks, her lips. His fingertips pushed wisps of hair away from her face, touched her cheeks, and rambled across her shoulders and down her arms as if he couldn't bear to be separated.

"Oh, Dan, what are we going to do?"

"We're going to have this baby, and as soon as medically possible, we're going to start a new one."

Hannah didn't argue now. Now wasn't the time. Now she'd be a coward and let herself be loved. Later was time enough to sort out the situation. Caught by a pain that was harder than the rest, she grabbed Dan's hand and pressed it against her stomach.

He could feel the movement, feel his child, feel an inexplicable surge of joy wash over him. This was man's ultimate experience. Never mind that the woman had the child, the man was a part of the creation and the delivery.

Hannah squeezed and panted. Dan panted. The others watched the two of them and knew that everything would be all right. Quietly they left the room. This was Dan and Hannah's moment, and they deserved to share it alone.

The doctor checked her one last time, nodded and backed away. "It won't be long now, Hannah, keep breathing. Hold what you've got, Dad, you're almost there."

Dan was leaning over Hannah, half lying on the birthing bed with her. She closed her eyes and forced herself to relax. Still wearing her flannel nightgown, she'd refused to allow the nurse to put her into one of those hospital gowns. The garment was twisted around her upper body, tugging at an awkward angle.

"Let me straighten your gown." Dan lifted her, pulling her face against his shoulder as he re-arranged the pillows and tried to arrange her gown. For a moment he allowed himself to hold her, to feel her lean against him willingly.

Not so fast, Dan, you'll spook her, and now is not the time to indulge in fantasies.

Carefully he laid her back against the pillows, adjusting the nightgown. He brushed her breasts and felt her shudder slightly. The full nipples pressed against the soft fabric—nipples that would soon nurse their child.

Dan didn't know why men always talked of childbirth in joking tones and masculine expressions, about how it was woman's work. To Dan it was beautiful. Hannah was beautiful. And more, it was sensual and incredibly arousing, not so much because he wanted to make love to Hannah, though he did and probably always would, but because it represented the most perfect moment between two people who loved each other.

This child was an expression of their love. Dan felt a tear slide down his cheek as he watched Hannah's eyes open.

"In my books the heroes used to cry. Then they didn't cry anymore; the public thought it took away from their strength."

"What do you think?"

"I think that it is beautiful and special and who cares what the books say. The readers don't know Dan Bailey."

"And you?"

The pain came again, and this time it didn't stop. Dan called for the doctor, who hurried in and donned his green mask. "We are about to meet Baby Clendening."

"Baby Bailey!" Dan corrected emotionally, and panted right along with Hannah.

It was a boy with a full head of thick dark hair and a little pink mouth that puckered and reached immediately for Hannah's breast.

"Definitely a Bailey," Dan said with pride as he watched the baby nurse.

Later, after Hannah had been cleaned up and given a clean bill of health, the doctor urged her to get some sleep. "Having a baby is probably the most exhilarating, demanding act a woman can subject her body to," Dr. Cross observed.

"Almost," Hannah whispered as she looked at Dan. "Almost."

It was the next morning when Dan's father and mother and his brother arrived. The hospital staff had to constantly admonish the family and friends of the romance editor whose room was being filled with flowers. The families were noisy and boisterous.

Hannah watched her father order Christmas portraits of every new mother on the floor. Dan's father presented them with a Christmas stocking filled with gifts. His brother gave out candy cigars, and Daisy brought all the women copies of a novel called *The Morning After*.

The baby didn't seem to mind. Daniel Carlton Bailey smiled and slept through being passed around like a treasure being rediscovered each time it was held. The new parents only had eyes for each other.

The hospital maintenance man kept adjusting the thermostat in Hannah's room. No, he had no explanation for the constant cloud of warm air that ebbed and flowed in the room, nor for the wild swings in temperature. He finally gave up and, in the middle of the Christmas season, brought a portable fan and connected it.

That night the hospital staff asked the guests to leave. Dan allowed himself to be pushed out the door. He didn't argue. He had a Christmas tree to put up, before his baby and his woman came home.

The next morning Dan helped get Hannah and the baby inside the cottage.

"Oh, Dan, a tree! It's beautiful. Thank you."

He turned on the lights. He'd stocked the kitchen, bought a Christmas tape for the stereo, and the nursery was ready.

It was, Dan discovered quickly, the parents who weren't prepared to deal with being alone with each other. If he could have taken Hannah to bed, he could have coped. He couldn't do that. The doctor had explained very carefully that they should wait for six weeks before being intimate.

He put Hannah to bed, gave her a chaste kiss, and sought refuge on the snowy deck. He'd gotten through eight months without Hannah. Six weeks ought to be a snap.

Hannah opened her bedroom door so that she could hear the baby when he cried. She walked to the window and peered out into the night, wondering where she and Dan were going from there. Everything that had happened had seemed to be out of control. It hadn't mattered when it was happening, but the future loomed big and uncertain.

How would they get through the next few days? What would she do about Dan Bailey? How could she cut him out of her life now that he'd become intimately involved again? How could she survive when he left the next time?

Eleven

When Danny cried out for his nine o'clock feeding, Hannah was still awake. She dashed quickly across the hall in an attempt to head off her self-appointed helper. She lifted the baby and sat down in the rocker, where she could nurse him more easily.

She hadn't been there more than a couple of minutes when Dan appeared, knelt by her side, and put another pair of his socks on her bare feet. Hannah tried to arrange her nightgown so that she was covered. Dan, still on his knees, leaned over and pulled the fabric away.

"Please," he said. "You're very beautiful, nursing our son. I want to watch."

Hannah didn't try to conceal herself anymore. She didn't know how to act around this new Dan. Half of her wanted to give in to the longing to accept his presence as some warm, wonderful fantasy. But he was so different from the brash, devil-may-care man who'd shared her house and her heart so many months ago. It would be too easy to begin to depend on him. And it would hurt too much when he left.

For he would go again, just as everyone she'd ever loved and trusted had. That was a certainty. But now she had this perfect little person who was such a part of her that he'd never go. She wouldn't let him, and she wouldn't let Dan make himself a part of the baby's life and leave him someday.

The baby made little slurping sounds as he nursed, his tiny fist laid against her breast. She decided she wouldn't fight Dan. Everything should be loving and good for their baby. Later, she'd face the inevitable.

Outside the wind blew, hurling snow and frozen mist against the glass. Inside the little house Hannah felt safe. Gradually the child grew quiet, and Hannah's own eyelids grew heavy. She was only half awake when Dan lifted the baby from her arms and returned him to his bed. She hardly roused when she felt Dan's arms around her. It seemed right to clasp her arms around his neck and allow him to take her back to her bed. It felt good to have someone care for her. She'd tell him in the morning that he didn't need to do that. But for now, it was comforting.

The next time the baby cried out, Dan brought him to the bed to be nursed. Hannah went back to sleep immediately. When she next woke, the sun was high in the sky. There was an indention on the pillow beside hers, and the baby's cries seemed very faint and far away.

Hannah came to her feet and ran into the hallway. The crib was empty. Down the stairs she dashed, catching her breath and gulping in air at the bottom. Dan was holding the baby in one arm and stirring eggs in the other.

"He let me give him that mixed-up stuff at six o'clock, but I don't think he's going to wait any longer for his real breakfast, Hannah. You take care of his, and I'll take care of yours."

He pulled a chair from the dining table and led her to it, handing her the baby at the same time he reached for the pair of socks on the counter. "I see now I'm going to have to pick up some more socks."

"Dan, I didn't want to say anything last night," Hannah said as she unbuttoned her gown and lifted the baby to nurse, "but you don't have to do this. I'll have to learn to take care of this child sooner or later on my own."

"You'll never have to look after this child on your own, Hannah. He's my son, and I'll be here for him. And," he added in a low voice, "I'll be here for you."

"Like you were during my pregnancy?" She wished she had the words back as soon as she'd said them.

There was a long silence. Dan pulled the skillet from the burner and stood, his shoulders tensed, his body totally still.

"I deserved that, Hannah. That and more. I would have come back if I'd known about the baby. I was coming back. I knew it every day I was gone."

"Then why didn't you?"

"I was afraid. You'd turned me and us into some kind of fantasy, and I've made such a mess of my personal relationships that I wasn't sure I could love you without screwing it up."

"You could have told me."

"I didn't think you'd understand."

"I wouldn't understand making a mess of personal relationships? You're talking to Hannah, who told her father to go take a flying leap because she was afraid she'd make another mistake and lose him too."

Dan turned slowly around, his eyes narrowed in uncertainty. "But you seemed to have worked it out. Carl and Gina were here for the baby's birth like any normal family."

"So was your family. I think your mother wanted to take Danny and me back to Augusta, like any normal family."

Dan was having trouble equating the two families and the two situations. But Hannah was right about one thing, his mother and father and his brother had come immediately, and they'd fallen in love with Hannah. Before they left, his father had taken Dan aside and confided that he thought Dan ought to marry her before somebody else did. But the biggest surprise had been when his brother fired him.

"You're too good a journalist to waste your time running my office, Dan. Get back where you belong, keeping all us politicians on the straight and narrow."

His mother simply had delivered a message: "Mattie said to tell you that she's getting old, but she'll be here after Christmas to see to the baby." Now Hannah was reinforcing how wrong he'd been.

"You see, Dan," she said, feeling her way through her words, "I've been doing a lot of thinking. Maybe the families are normal. Maybe we're the ones who aren't."

Dan looked around the little house with its Christmas tree, its warm fire in the fireplace, the coffee perking on the stove, and Hannah nursing their child.

"Hannah, this looks pretty normal to me. I like everything I see. I like it very much."

Hannah lifted the baby to her shoulder and patted him gently on his back until she was rewarded with a big burp. "So do I," she admitted, "But we mustn't let ourselves be carried away with temporary emotion. We met and got caught up in some kind of heated whirlwind. We can't let that happen again."

"Speak for yourself," he said softly. "From the moment I stepped back through that door, I've felt it starting up again. It was all I could do to hold you in my arms last night and not—touch you. I don't know if it's us or this cottage, but if that doctor hadn't told me I couldn't, we'd be making love right now."

Hannah's gasp was audible. "No, Dan. I won't have this happen again. I can't physically force you to leave, but I won't—I can't lose control again." She snuggled her chin against the baby and held him close. "We have to examine the situation logically."

"I've tried. I promise. From the time I put you to bed last night until the baby woke, I walked this room trying to be logical." He turned back to the stove and replaced the skillet on the fire. "I've come to the conclusion that there's no fighting it. Forget logic, Hannah. All logic went out the window when we met."

She didn't want to agree, yet she had no argument against what he was saying. She came to her feet and started up the stairs. "I have to change the baby. Then I'll come back downstairs and we'll talk."

"Hey," Dan called out, "I changed him last night. Be careful, he's dangerous if you get too close at the wrong time."

She couldn't hold back a smile at the picture of Dan changing the baby's diaper.

"He's pretty special, Hannah," Dan was saying. "You couldn't create anything that wasn't."

Hannah agreed. Create they could do, it was talking that they had trouble with. And having a normal relationship where they could believe in and depend on each other. And sharing their son, without sharing a bed.

"Now, about that talking." Hannah sat on a stool and spooned sugar into the cup of coffee Dan had poured. "I'm ready to listen."

Dan nodded and pulled up an adjoining stool.

"So long," she added, "as you stay on the other side of the counter."

With a rueful smile Dan moved around the

counter to the kitchen side, directly opposite Hannah. He took an appreciative look at her and thought about sharing breakfast with her every morning. He picked up his fork.

Hannah desperately wished that she knew what to say to him. She'd tried to fortify herself by changing into a pair of corduroy slacks and a blue cable-knit sweater. Her feet finally fit her shoes again, though she did miss the soft warmth of Dan's socks. But that wasn't helping. He was undressing her with his eyes, and she could feel her response.

"Stop that!" she snapped.

"Ah, sure. Do you mean the coffee drinking, or the egg eating?"

"What?"

Hannah knew she'd made a mistake. With Dan across the narrow counter from her she couldn't avoid his eyes, which immediately caught and held her gaze.

"You said 'stop that,' " he explained.

"Oh, I think I was talking to myself. I often do that when I have a problem I'm trying to work out."

"I've never heard you before."

"That's because you're not with me when I'm alone. I mean, that's the only time I talk to myself. I used to tell myself stories when I was a little girl. Nobody heard me then either." There was an odd break in her voice.

"You were very lonely, weren't you?"

"I suppose. I mean, I didn't know I was, but yes, I would have liked to have someone real—talk to me."

"Well, you won't have to worry about that. Mattie will talk your ear off."

"Mattie?"

Dan forced his attention back to his plate, away from eyes so blue that he thought of sunshine and picnics and baseball. All the things that families did. Of a little boy with short fat legs pulling handfuls of wildflowers and taking them to his mother. Of the father sprinkling them across her body.

"Dan, how is Mattie going to talk my ear off?"

"Oh, Mother is sending her after Christmas, to help with the baby. You won't have to look for a nanny. Of course, we're going to have to work out a place for her to stay. What about a cot in the baby's room?"

"But Dan, Mattie?"

"What's wrong with Mattie? She raised me."

"I know. I guess that's what bothers me. I got the idea that you were pretty unhappy as a child too."

"I wasn't unhappy because nobody loved me. I was . . . difficult. Whatever anybody wanted me to do, I did the opposite. I didn't understand then, but I think I was too different from my father and my brother. They didn't know how to deal with a kid who wanted to investigate the dog pound because the dogcatcher used a choke chain to drag the strays to the truck. Then there was the time I accused the lunchroom cook of absconding with all the ice cream bars because they'd disappeared from the grammar school menu."

"Took ice cream off the menu? Why?"

"Well, I'll admit that some of us used the sticks

from the ice cream as launching pads for the peas we didn't eat. But it was the principle of the thing.

"Then I embarrassed my father when he was running for judge by printing an editorial in the school newspaper about sex education."

"A crusader from the start. Don't all journalists see themselves as crusaders?"

"Yes, it's just taken me a long time to understand that judges and senators feel the same way. I go about it one way and they do it in another. And if it hadn't been for Mattie, I might have been in that prison for real."

"I can believe that you'd go to jail for something you believed in, all right. I might do the same."

"Somewhere along the way, like a lot of others who hold the power of the written word, I became invincible. The public deserves to know, which translated into revealing the truth, no matter who it hurt. You can excuse a lot of actions in the name of exposing the bad guys, but you don't forget it."

Hannah finished off her coffee and poured herself a glass of juice. They were alone and they were talking, and for a moment the passion that flared between them seemed to be under control.

Dan stood and walked to the glass doors overlooking the sound. "The sun is shining, but it's an illusion, isn't it. The wind is cold and the water is almost pure ice. I wonder where the swans are?"

"My grandfather used to tell me that they went to the Carolinas in the winter. It was warm enough to survive, but still cold enough for them to think they were home. They found their own promise of tomorrow."

"Like you finding me," Dan said.

"You lost me on that one."

"You found me and you took me home, into your fantasy world where you protected me. There was only one problem. I didn't trust myself to fall in love. I was afraid that if I stayed, I'd hurt you. So I left and I forced myself to stay away."

"How, why would you hurt me, Dan?"

"You told me once that your father came for you and you sent him away. You'd made your life without him, and by the time he wanted you, you'd filled his place with something you could trust to be permanent. I thought perhaps I was too much like your father."

"Did I send you away the night you came back?"

"No, but you wanted to. If you hadn't gone into labor, I'd have been history. I've already been the past. Now I want to be the future."

"The future will have to take care of itself. This isn't a romance novel, Dan. I don't have a nice, neat synopsis that tells me how we resolve conflict and get to the 'happily ever after.' "

"At least we know what the conflict is," he said softly.

"We do?" She gave him a puzzled look. "And what do you think it is?"

"This, and what to do about it."

He kissed her. Not chastely as in a nice hello. Not on the forehead in comfort. Not on the cheek as a thank-you. But as a man kisses a woman he cares about, he needs, he desires, he cherishes.

Like a woman he loves.

Breathless, she finally managed to pull away.

"I'm not the man I was. I'm your promise being kept. And I'm not leaving you or our baby or our bed."

"But, Dan, nothing is resolved. I mean we can't. What will we do?"

"We'll do what any other husband and wife do after the wife gives birth, we'll wait."

"But we aren't husband and wife." *And how on earth are we going to wait?* Even now her pulse was racing and her veins had turned into liquid fire. Dan wasn't managing much better. She could feel his heart beating like a tom-tom in the middle of a Sioux attack.

"We will be, as soon as we can set up the wedding. Now, can you hold down the fort here? I have to go out and find a job."

"A job? You're going looking for a job during Christmas week?"

"Yes. You'll have to go into the city, so I figure I'll have to stay close by so that I can keep an eye on Danny and Mattie."

But it wasn't the eyes he intended to keep on Mattie that drove Hannah wild. It was the eyes he watched her with, and the hands that soothed, touched, and caressed. And the nights they lay side by side until neither could stand it any longer and she moved into his embrace, welcoming his kisses, driving them both wild until he'd leave the room and spend the rest of the night on the couch.

At least once a day Hannah bundled up the baby, and she and Dan took a walk down to the village. They held hands, laughed, and talked. She learned that his favorite authors were John Grisham and Robert R. McCammon. He learned that she hated oysters and adored chocolate. Being close was safe in public, and they let themselves enjoy being together. It was when they were back in the cottage that the rooms seem to shrink.

The local bookstore had sold out of the January Fantasy the first week, and when the book chain's best-seller lists came out they learned that *The Morning After* had made the list at number one and had stayed on for the third week.

Christmas Eve was sweet agony. Hannah bought a goose, then gave it away. It looked too much like a swan, and she couldn't bear to think that it might have a soulmate somewhere grieving. Instead she baked a ham. Dan prepared a sweet potato casserole according to one of Mattie's recipes and put the green beans on to cook while Hannah unwrapped the fruitcake Daisy had sent.

Dan took the baby upstairs and bedded him down for the night. While he was doing that, Hannah put the finishing touches on their Christmas Eve feast.

She brought the wineglasses to the table as Dan returned. Dan reached for the wine at the same moment she did. Their hands touched and jerked away.

Even though they'd managed to work out a certain routine that kept them from direct contact for most of the day, the ever-growing awareness was always there. The harder they tried to ignore it, the stronger it became. Hannah decided that she could walk through her house in the dark and not touch a stick of furniture, she'd had so much experience looking at the floor to avoid seeing Dan.

"I'm sorry, Hannah. It's rough being here and not being able to touch you. Maybe this was a bad idea."

"No, you've been wonderful with the baby. And I've liked having you here, even if . . ."

"Next week Mattie will be here."

"Yes."

"And we can both—" He seemed to be having a hard time finding the right word. "We can both get back to work."

"Yes," she agreed quietly. "Of course, that's what we'd planned. Having Mattie is better than a stranger. I'll be able to go into the city for at least two days a week, maybe three."

"Danny will do fine. And I'll be in and out, between assignments. They're ready for me to come back to the magazine. But I haven't told them I'd come. I can't leave you until the doctor says that you both are all right."

"Yes. Then we'll be able—I mean, things will be back to normal." To her great surprise, Hannah felt tears welling up in her eyes. She was about to cry, and she didn't know why. She didn't understand the tight, hopeless feeling that seemed to be strangling the air right out of her lungs. Her throat hurt from muscles tensed.

She felt those hot, fuzzy tarantula legs scurrying along her spine. Her knees seemed perpetually weak ever since she'd had the baby, though the doctor assured her that time would fix everything. She couldn't tell him that time couldn't fix her problem because it had nothing to do with childbirth. Before she dropped it, Hannah set the ham down on the table with a *thunk*.

"We'd better eat," Hannah said.

"Shall I pour the wine?"

"Please."

Hannah swallowed hard. At the rate they were going, they'd be toasting Christmas breakfast instead of Santa's arrival. She studied the burned edges of the soufflé baking dish as Dan opened the bottle and poured the wine.

He lifted his glass. "What shall we drink to?"

"I don't know, next year?"

"That's what you drink to on New Year's Eve, but I think you're right." He lifted his glass, "To new beginnings and promises kept. Merry Christmas, Hannah. And—will you marry me?"

Hannah stared at the Christmas tree. As she turned her goblet it acted like a prism and sent flecks of colored starlight across the door and beyond, to the deck.

"Are you sure, Dan?"

"I've never been as sure of anything in my life."

But what about me? she thought. *What will happen to us if we love each other? Can we do it and survive? Can I not marry Dan? Can I stop loving him? No.*

Hannah replied in the only way possible for her. She said, "Of course I will, Dan."

Dan touched his glass to hers, then set it on the table. "You know I have to kiss you."

"Please don't, Dan. It isn't that I don't want you to, but kissing makes it so hard."

"Hard is a part of my permanent physical condition, Hannah. I'm sorry, but I must touch you, just a little."

She couldn't resist him. She couldn't keep from responding. When his hands reached beneath her sweater she followed his lead, and soon they were lying on the rug before the fire touching and kissing and fueling the fire with their heat.

"Dan, we can't. Oh, Dan."

"Hannah, I can't put myself inside you, but there are some things we *can* do. Some things we have to do, now, tonight." And they did.

After they fed the baby, they opened their Christmas gifts. There was a football and a baseball and cowboy guns for the baby. Hannah's gift to Dan was a year's supply of brightly colored socks. Dan's gift to her was matching house slippers for the two of them.

"You know," Hannah said dreamily as she lay in the circle of his arms, "Daisy always said that I'm a sucker for Christmas. If an author has her characters decorate a Christmas tree, she's got me. All she has to do for me to buy the book is have them make love under the tree. I think it's the emotional promise of love that gets to me."

"You mean a Christmas tree is all it takes?"

"Well, it doesn't hurt to have weddings and babies added to the 'happily ever after.'"

"Exactly my thinking. I don't suppose it matters if we got the order slightly wrong, does it?"

"Not at all. We're still a gold-star five."

Later, the *Jeffersonian Ledger* carried the announcement in the Jeff Notes column on the women's page.

> Romance editor Hannah Clendening and journalist Dan Bailey were married on Saturday evening. The ceremony, smooth and serene on the surface, concealed a comedy of errors along the way.
>
> The minister had throat surgery three days before the wedding and had to have an interpreter; the organist got the flu the morning of the ceremony and had to be replaced. The photographer, a man with only one eye, had an eye infection and had to take the pictures wearing a pair of dark glasses. An icy parking lot caused a wreck, which blocked the exit, and Daisy, the best woman, forgot the rings.
>
> To make matters worse, the baby began to cry, and the wedding had to stop while he was fed. The honeymoon was to be very unusual, because, according to a reliable source, they were sharing it with a Miss Rachel Kimbel and a Mr. Razor Cody.

But to Hannah and Dan, the wedding was perfect. With both families coaching them on their vows and Daisy openly ogling Captain Joe, they decided that a very good time had been had by all.

Later, when the last guest had pushed out the door, Mattie took the baby and went to bed, leaving Hannah and Dan alone at last.

"Would you like another glass of champagne?" Dan asked.

"No, I'm practically flying now."

"Of course, I don't have much experience with weddings," Dan said, "but I thought everything went pretty well."

"Absolutely. Especially the part where you promised to love, honor, and cherish."

"Cherish," he said with a wide, sensual smile. "I think I like the idea of that. If you could fly up those stairs, I'll bring the champagne. I think we've waited long enough to start cherishing, don't you?"

"It wasn't my idea to sleep apart after Mattie arrived," she said, and started up the stairs.

"No, it wasn't mine either. Mattie and Daisy ganged up on me. Something about abstinence being a virtue and the best way for me to stay alive in a house filled with three women. They thought it was romantic." Dan followed, watching her lovely legs move ahead of him. "I didn't trust myself to wait for the doctor's okay."

"What did Mattie say tonight?"

"She said that she snores so loud, she can't hear herself think, and not to worry about Danny, she's got him covered for the night."

At that moment, from behind Mattie's door, they

heard a noise that would have put Paul Bunyan's tree-sawing to shame.

Hannah looked at Dan, who began to snicker. He pulled Hannah into the bedroom, closed the door, switched on the stereo, and turned down the lights. He filled their glasses once more and handed one to Hannah.

"Now, Mrs. Bailey, your husband wants to make a few vows of his own. I love you. I will always be here for you. I'll share your joys and your troubles. From this moment through forever I'll be a promise kept."

"Oh, Dan. I love you so much. But you don't have to promise to be here always. I know your job will take you away, and I understand."

"Not anymore, Mrs. Bailey. I have a surprise. This is my wedding gift to you." He pulled an envelope from his coat and handed it to her.

Hannah opened it. "A bill of sale? For the *Ledger*? You bought the newspaper?"

"I did. Your father sold it to me. He wanted to make it a wedding gift, but I refused. If a thing comes too easy, it isn't always appreciated. I wanted to struggle to make it work."

"Oh, Dan. I have something for you too. Do you want it now or later?"

He began to remove her clothes, kissing her between each button. "I don't know. Give me a hint?"

She followed his actions, button for button. "Let's just say that if you fail as a newspaper man, I have your next career all lined up."

"I thought loving you was going to be a full-time job."

"Not if your fans have anything to say about it."

"Fans?"

Hannah danced away and picked up a shopping bag beside the bed. "Here they are, Dan, letters to Razor Cody, from thousand of readers who want to worship your body." Holding her champagne glass in one hand, she turned the bag upside down and poured the letters on the bed with the other. "A toast, Dan. You're Hannah's most famous hunk."

He looked at the pile in amazement. "Readers?"

"And a few writers who want you on their book covers."

"And what did you tell them, Madam Editor?"

"I told them that I had an exclusive contract on your services—forever."

They'd been caught up in a firestorm when they first made love. Then later, restraining their needs, they'd learned that love was more than physical. It was commitment, a promise for tomorrow.

Now Dan placed their glasses on the bureau and took Hannah into his arms. This night, their lovemaking would be slow, gentle, and special.

"Cherish," Dan said. "I like that word."

"Cherish," Hannah echoed. "I think it must be the best kind of love."

"Can we love each other for another fifty years?" Dan asked.

"And more," Hannah said with a satisfied sigh.

"Well, I don't know about that, I'll be an old man. Maybe I won't be able to keep up."

"Sure you will. I have it on good authority. If Razor can do it, so can you."

"What about Razor? I never got past the cover of the book, and you never did tell me how the story ended."

"I know," she said with a smile. "And I don't think I'm going to. If you want to find out what happened to Razor and Rachel, you have to read the book for yourself. Tonight the only story we're telling is the one about Hannah and Dan."

Downstairs, in the portrait hanging over the mantel, there was a moment when the aura around Razor and Rachel seemed to intensify. And if anybody had been watching, they'd have sworn that the expression in the couple's eyes seemed more intense.

Upstairs, Hannah returned Dan's kiss. "On the other hand," she said breathlessly, "maybe I'll show you what to expect tonight and *The Morning After*."

THE EDITOR'S CORNER

There's no better way to get into the springtime mood than to read the six fabulous LOVESWEPTs coming your way. Humorous and serious, sexy and tender, with heroes and heroines you'll long remember, these novels are guaranteed to turn May into a merry month indeed.

Leading this great lineup is Linda Jenkins with **TALL ORDER**, LOVESWEPT #612. At 6'7", Gray Kincaid is certainly one long, tall hunk, just the kind of man statuesque Garnet Brindisi has been waiting for. And with her flamboyant, feisty manner, she's just the one-woman heat wave who can finally melt the cool reserve of the ex-basketball star called the Iceman. . . . Linda's writing makes the courtship between this unlikely couple a very exciting one to follow.

Please welcome Janis Reams Hudson, bestselling and award-winning author of historical and contemporary romances, and her first LOVESWEPT, **TRUTH OR DARE**, #613. In this touching story, Rachel Fredrick dons a shapeless dress, wig, and glasses, convinced the disguise will forever hide her real identity—and notorious past. She doesn't count on her boss, Jared Morgan, discovering the truth and daring her to let him heal her pain. Enjoy one of New Faces of '93!

STROKE BY STROKE, LOVESWEPT #614 by Patt Bucheister, is how Turner Knight wants to convince Emma Valerian she's the only woman for him. For two years she's been the best paralegal Turner has ever worked with—but the way his body heats up whenever she walks into his office has nothing to do with business. Now she's quitting and Turner can at last confess his hunger and desire. We know you'll treasure this stirring romance from Patt.

In her new LOVESWEPT, Diane Pershing gives you a dangerously sexy hero who offers nothing but **SATISFACTION**, #615. An irresistibly wicked rebel, T. R. is every woman's dream, but Kate O'Brien has vowed never to fall for another heartbreaker. Still, how can she resist a man who warns her she'll be bored with a safe, predictable guy, then dares her to play with his fire? Diane tells this story with breathtaking passion.

Prepare to thrill to romance as you read Linda Warren's second LOVESWEPT, **SWEPT AWAY**, #616. Jake Marlow never intended to return to the family whale-watching business, but he smells sabotage in the air—and he has to consider every possible suspect, including Maria Santos, the exquisitely beautiful fleet manager. The sparks of desire between these two can probably set fire to the ocean! A powerful romance from a powerful storyteller.

Adrienne Staff returns to LOVESWEPT with **PLEASURE IN THE SAND**, #617. In this heart-stirring romance, Jody Conners's nightmare of getting lost at sea turns into a dream when she's rescued by movie star Eric Ransom. Years ago Hollywood's gorgeous bad boy had suddenly dropped out of the public eye, and when he takes Jody to his private island, she discovers only she has the power to coax him—and his guarded heart—out of hiding. Welcome back, Adrienne!

On sale this month from Bantam are three fabulous novels. Teresa Medeiros follows her bestselling **HEATHER**

AND VELVET with **ONCE AN ANGEL**, a captivating historical romance that sweeps from the wilds of an exotic paradise to the elegance of Victorian England. Emily Claire Scarborough sails halfway around the world to find Justin Connor, the man who had cheated her out of her inheritance—and is determined to make him pay with nothing less than his heart.

With **IN A ROGUE'S ARMS**, Virginia Lynn delivers an enchanting, passion-filled retelling of the beloved Robin Hood tale, set in Texas in the 1870s. When Cale Hardin robs Chloe Mitchell's carriage, she swears to take revenge . . . even as she finds herself succumbing to the fascination of this bold and brazen outlaw.

IN A ROGUE'S ARMS is the first book in Bantam's ONCE UPON A TIME romances—passionate historical romances inspired by beloved fairy tales, myths, and legends, penned by some of the finest romance authors writing today, and featuring the most beautiful front and stepback covers. Be sure to look for **PROMISE ME MAGIC** by Patricia Camden, inspired by "Puss in Boots," coming in the summer of 1993, and **CAPTURE THE NIGHT** by Geralyn Dawson, inspired by "Beauty and the Beast," coming in the late fall of 1993.

Favorite LOVESWEPT author Fran Baker makes a spectacular debut in FANFARE with **THE LADY AND THE CHAMP**, which Julie Garwood has already praised as "Unforgettable . . . a warm, wonderful knockout of a book." You'll cheer as Maureen Bryant and Jack Ryan risk anything—even Jack's high-stakes return to the ring—to fight for their chance at love.

Bantam/Doubleday/Dell welcomes Jane Feather with the Doubleday hardcover edition of **VIRTUE**. Set in Regency England, this highly sensual tale brings together a strong-willed beauty who makes her living at the gaming tables and the arrogant nobleman determined to best her with passion.

Happy reading!

With warmest wishes,

Nita Taublib
Associate Publisher
LOVESWEPT and FANFARE

Don't miss these fabulous
Bantam
Women's Fiction
titles
on sale in MARCH

ONCE AN ANGEL
by Teresa Medeiros

IN A ROGUE'S ARMS
by Virginia Brown
writing as Virginia Lynn

THE LADY AND THE CHAMP
by Fran Baker

In hardcover from Doubleday,
VIRTUE
by Jane Feather
author of
THE EAGLE AND THE DOVE

ONCE AN ANGEL
by Teresa Medeiros
author of HEATHER AND VELVET

From the enthralling Teresa Medeiros comes this irresistible new historical romance that ranges from the wilds of an exotic paradise to the elegance of Victorian England.

The last thing Justin Connor expected to find washed up on the wild shores of New Zealand was a young woman asleep on the sand, curled like a child beneath the moonlight. Though fiercely protective of the haven he had found on this island paradise, Justin was compelled to rescue this mysterious refugee, little realizing she would shatter his peace forever with her defiant courage, her vivid beauty, and the memories she stirred of a past best forgotten. . . .

Orphaned, cheated of her inheritance, Emily had sailed halfway around the world to find the man who had promised her father to take care of her—and instead had left her a charity case in an English boarding school. She never dreamed she'd be tossed by the pounding surf practically at his feet, or that she'd find him a disturbingly handsome recluse with the look of a pirate . . . and a disarming tenderness in his amber-flecked eyes. Confused by conflicting emotions, Emily was determined to make Justin pay for her years of loneliness with nothing less than his heart. . . .

Emily burrowed into the thin mattress, her mind tugging greedily at the blurred edges of sleep. She despised waking up. Despised the sleet tapping at the tiny attic window, the wash water frozen in her basin, the prospect of crawling down the steep stairs to teach French to wealthy little brats who didn't know their *demitasses* from their *derrières* and who teased her mercilessly because her dress was two years too small. Groaning, she fumbled for a pillow to pull over her head. Perhaps if she hid long enough, Tansy would come tapping on the door with a mug of steaming black coffee smuggled out from under Cook's bulbous nose.

Her groping search yielded no pillow. A new sensation crept over her, a feeling utterly delicious and so foreign to her gloomy attic that she wanted to weep at its beauty.

Warmth.

She slowly opened her eyes. The sun fanned tingling fingers across her face. She lay there, stunned, basking in its heat, enveloped in its healing rays. She closed her eyes against the dazzling shaft of light. When she opened them again, a twisted green face hung only an inch above her own, its pointed teeth bared in a ferocious grimace.

She shrieked and scrambled backward, groping for a weapon. Her fingers curled around the first blunt object they could find. As her back slammed into a wall, dust exploded, setting her off on a quaking chain of sneezes.

"Now look what you've done, Trinl. You've frightened the poor girl. I dare say she's never seen a savage before."

Emily wiped her streaming eyes. Now two faces were peering at her. One was still green, but the other was round and decidedly English. It was clicking its tongue and shaking its side-whiskers like a great overgrown hamster.

The fierce green face loomed nearer. "How do you do, miss? The sheer luminosity of your countenance beguiles me. I take extreme delight in welcoming you, our most charming breast."

The round face pinkened. Emily gaped. The savage's words had come rolling out in deep, resonant tones as if he'd just strolled from the hallowed corridors of Cambridge, his feathered cloak swinging around his shoulders. Emily realized his teeth were bared not in a snarl, but in a beaming smile. Nor was he entirely green. Deep furrows of jade had been tattooed in his honey-colored skin in elaborate curls and soaring wings.

A soft groan came out of the shadows. "Not breast, Trinl. *Guest.*"

She squinted into the corner, but the sunlight had blinded her. She could make out only a vague shape.

The tattooed man stretched out a hand. She recoiled and smacked it away. "I'll keep my breast to myself, thank you. I'm not a simpering ninny for some native Lothario to ravish."

The savage threw back his head. His musical laughter rocked the small hut.

"Did I say something amusing?" she asked the hamster. Her head was starting to pound and she was wishing even more desperately for that coffee.

"Oh, dear, I'm afraid so. You see—the Maori don't ravish their victims." He leaned forward and whispered, "They eat them."

Emily felt herself go the same color as the snorting native. She pressed herself to the wall. "Stay away from me. I'm warning the both of you. I wasn't kicked out of every girls' school in England for nothing." Emily disliked lying. She much preferred to embellish the truth.

She attacked the air with her makeshift weapon. The native danced backward. Narrowing her eyes in what she hoped was a menacing fashion, she said, "That's right. I know how to use this thing."

"What a comfort," came a dry voice from the corner. "If Penfeld ever decides to stop serving tea long enough to dust, you'll be of great service."

Emily glanced down to discover she was threatening a cannibal with a feather duster. Her cheeks burned.

A man unfolded himself from the shadows with lanky grace. He stepped into a beam of sunlight, tilting back a battered panama hat with one finger.

Their eyes met and Emily remembered everything. She remembered swimming until her arms and legs had turned leaden and her head bobbed under the water with each stroke. She remembered crawling onto the beach and collapsing in the warm sand. Then her memories hazed—a man's mouth melted tenderly into hers, his dark-lashed eyes the color of sunlight on honey.

Emily gazed up into those eyes. Their depths were a little sad, a trifle mocking. She couldn't tell if they mocked her or himself. She forced her gaze down from his, then wished she hadn't.

Her throat constricted. His physical presence was as daunting as a blow. She had never seen quite so much man. The sheer volume of his sun-bronzed skin both shocked and fascinated her. In London the men swathed themselves in layers of clothing from the points of their high starched collars to the tips of their polished shoes. Shaggy whiskers shielded any patch of skin that risked exposure.

But this man wore nothing but sheared-off dungarees that clung low on his narrow hips. The chiseled muscles of his chest and calves drank in the sunlight. To Emily's shocked eyes, he might as well have been naked.

Another unwelcome memory returned—damp sand clinging to her own bare skin. The pulse in her throat throbbed to mortified life. She glanced down to find herself wrapped in the voluminous folds of a man's frock coat. The sleeves hung far below her hands, nearly enveloping the duster.

"My man Penfeld was kind enough to lend you his coat."

The husky scratch of the stranger's voice sent shivers down her spine. An endearing lilt had been layered over his clipped

English, flavoring it with an exotic cadence. She had heard similar accents in Melbourne.

Disconcerted to find her thoughts read so neatly, she shot him a nasty look. A dazzling smile split the somber black of his stubbled chin. Dear Lord, the amiable wretch had kissed her! What other liberties had he taken while she lay in his embrace? Dropping the offensive duster, Emily buried her fists in the coat and hugged herself, fighting a sudden chill.

A **Once Upon a Time**
Romance

IN A ROGUE'S ARMS

by Virginia Brown
writing as Virginia Lynn

**From the bestselling author of LYON'S PRIZE and A
TOUCH OF HEAVEN, this passion-filled retelling of
"Robin Hood" is the story of a Texas outlaw and the
pampered niece of his ruthless enemy.**

*One moment Chloe was lost in daydreams about her new Texas
home; the next she was holding on for dear life as gunfire echoed
and her uncle's carriage came rumbling to a halt! Before she could
even draw a breath, the fair-haired beauty found herself on the
ground. . . . and in the clutches of a bold and brazen outlaw known
as "the Baron." Daring and dangerous, he took what he wanted
from the wealthy, and now as she watched in helpless rage, he
turned his hungry gaze upon her. . . .*

*For Cale Hardin, humiliation and empty pockets were a modest
revenge for the crimes committed by Chloe's uncle, who made
his money from the misery of others. Yet when the banker's
niece came tumbling out of the carriage all spitting fury and
white petticoats, Cale knew he at last had his foe where he
wanted him. But what he didn't know, what he could never
foresee, was his own reaction to the fair Chloe, for when he
took her in his arms, he'd never want to let her go. . . .*

"Kill me," she moaned, "I don't care, but I cannot get up and walk another step tonight. You'll have to drag my lifeless body somewhere to dispose of it. I can't move. I won't move. I hate you for being such a monster."

Cale sat his horse and watched her. Saddle leather creaked, and the wind sloughed through the trees with a swishing sound.

Chloe waited. Finally she lifted her head, and found him gazing at her with something close to sympathy. Then she thought she must be mistaken, because his expression was once more cold and remote. That brief impression, however, unnerved her.

Since she'd awakened to find him touching her, her feelings toward him had subtly altered. This smoky-eyed outlaw had somehow done much more than just touch her body. He'd awakened something inside her, some demon that pricked her at odd moments with the memory of how it had felt to be caressed intimately, to have his hands on her.

It was as if a stranger inhabited her body, some wicked creature without morals or pride and craved the sensuous feel of a man's hands. Disturbed by the unfamiliar emotions he provoked, Chloe struggled to recapture her original revulsion. He was a rogue and an outlaw and no decent woman could feel pleasure in his arms.

Chloe staggered to her feet, facing Cale and wondering why he kept staring at her with those bullet-gray eyes so unreadable in the shadows. Nothing showed on his face, no emotion, no reaction. It was unnerving. She stepped down from the porch.

"If you try to run," he said quietly, "I'll put the rope around you again. And it will stay there." His voice was flat and calm, but she knew he meant what he said.

God, he was so close, much too close for comfort. Why did he keep looking at her like that? Frozen, she could only stare up at him and wait.

Silence stretched tautly, and she couldn't look away. Dark shadows blurred around him as he swung down from his horse and crossed to her. One hand reached out to snag in her hair, tilting her head back so that she couldn't escape his gaze.

"You're poison, Chloe Mitchell," he muttered. "Sweet poison . . ."

There was only time for a gasp and grab at his arms before Cale was pushing her back against the porch. The edge caught her behind the knees, and when she went back in a graceless sprawl, he went with her. Taut muscles under her fingers felt like steel, inflexible and immovable.

Fear fluttered like a trapped bird in her chest. His hard, lean body felt like steel against hers, holding her down, his hands on each side of her head. He looked down at her for a long moment, his expression unreadable, his eyes veiled by his lashes. Chloe held to his arms as if drowning.

"Why are you doing this?" she asked when he pressed his mouth to her throat.

His head lifted. Satan's own eyes looked back at her, tarnished silver smoldering with sensuality beneath an inky brush of thick lashes. The breath caught in her throat, and something lurched through her. Excitement? Anticipation?

As her lips parted to protest, his mouth came over them. Then he was forcing her lips apart farther with his tongue, a heated invasion that thrust all thought of protest from her mind. A sound strangled in the back of her throat, surprise or excitement, or maybe a mix of the two.

His grip tightened on her, fingers spreading over her scalp as he held her head still for his tongue to explore her mouth. She moaned, unwilling participation. He seemed to like that as he explored more, drawing the breath from her lungs and sending small bursts of sensation licking along her stretched nerve ends.

When his head finally lifted, leaving her breathless and still and dazzled with reaction, his mouth flattened in a moody smile.

"I wanted you that first day I saw you."

"And now?" she got out, her voice a whisper of sound.

He released her and stood up, uncoiling his lead body into a straight line. He studied her gravely. "And now I have you."

"Unforgettable . . . a warm, wonderful knockout of a book." —Julie Garwood

THE LADY AND THE CHAMP
by Fran Baker

Walking into that fight gym was the hardest thing Maureen Bryant had ever done, but the painful memories of the father she barely knew vanished the instant she beheld the fighter in the ring. All sculpted muscles and sun-bronzed skin, Jack Ryan was the most gorgeous man she'd ever seen, a sleek Adonis whose powerful physique left her weak. But she knew better than to surrender her heart to another man who'd give her up without a second thought.

One look at the gym's new owner and Jack Ryan almost went down for the count. Yet he knew that beneath her elegant exterior, Sully's long-lost daughter couldn't have a heart. Sully had been the father that Jack had always needed, the only person who could have turned a troubled youth around. Now Jack was ready to do anything— even climb back into the ring for the biggest challenge of his life— to save Sully's gym from the woman who would let it die. But even as he put on the gloves, something told him the real fight would be in letting Maureen go. . . .

The man who climbed into the ring at that very same moment stopped her cold.

He wore a plastic headguard, black satin trunks, and nothing in between. His smooth, sun-bronzed neck flowed into shoulders that were about a yard wide and biceps that looked as round and firm as green apples. His red-gloved hands flashed like thunderbolts when he started shadowboxing, pummeling his invisible opponent with a furious flurry of rights and lefts.

Maureen abhorred violence, and she found no redeeming social value in blood sports of any kind. Standing ringside, though, she suddenly saw a brutal Renaissance beauty in the boxer's sculpted physique and athletic prowess, a beauty that was as frightening as it was fascinating to behold.

"He's all yours," said a gravelly voice just beside her.

Startled, she jumped, then spun to find she'd been joined by a balding little man with a big smile. She tilted her head, the better to hear him. "I beg your pardon?"

He pointed the unlit cigar he was carrying toward the muscular giant in the center ring. "I said, 'he's all yours.' "

"*Mine?*"

"You're Maureen, aren't you?"

Momentarily taken aback, she could only nod.

"Then you own his contract."

Now she shook her head. "But—"

"And he owes you a fight."

Puzzled, she swung her gaze back to the subject of this bizarre discussion. The commercial developer had mentioned something to the effect that she would probably have to buy out some old boxer's contract when she sold the gym. But the man in the ring looked to be in his prime.

"How old is he?" she asked, still grappling with this surprising news.

"Thirty-eight."

"That's not old!" Only three years older than she, in fact.

"It is for a fighter."

Maureen examined the boxer a little closer, looking for flaws. He hadn't gone to fat, as aging athletes are wont to do. To the contrary, his inverted triangle of a chest tapered to a trim waist and, judging from the way that black satin fabric draped itself over them, taut hips.

Nor did he seem to have "lost his legs," to quote a former Royals' baseball player whose trophy room she had recently redecorated. Quite the opposite, in fact. The boxer's powerful thighs and balustrade calves provided the perfect blend of balance and leverage as he danced backward and forward and sideways across the canvas in a pugilistic ballet that literally left her breathless.

She fanned her face, which suddenly felt warm, with her flat ivory clutch purse. Then she caught herself and, quickly dropping her hand, asked a question off the top of her head. "How much does he weigh?"

"One-ninety." Her sidekick hitched up his pants, and she was surprised he didn't strangle himself. "That's stripped, of course."

Her voice, when she managed to find it again, came out in a squeak. "Of course."

"You oughtta put another fifteen pounds on him before you fight him again."

Maureen pointedly ignored that piece of advice. "Has he ever won anything?"

"The Golden Gloves title."

"I thought that was for amateurs." Even as she said it, she wondered what hidden corner of her mind that tidbit had popped out of.

"It is."

"Well, I meant professionally."

"Seventeen KO's in eighteen fights."

"KO's?" She frowned, trying to put words to the strangely familiar term.

"Knockouts."

"Right." Now she smiled, inordinately pleased to have that clarified. "What happened in the eighteenth fight?"

For the first time since he'd walked up and started talking

to her, the man hesitated. He clamped the cold cigar between his teeth with fingers that were short and stubby and stained tobacco-brown. Then he chewed the stogie from one side of his mouth to the other before removing it and flicking the nonexistent ash onto the floor.

"Technical knockout," he said in a clipped tone.

She tipped her head inquiringly. "Which means?"

"The referee called the fight in the second round."

"Why?" She saw the reluctance in his pale blue eyes and realized she probably wasn't going to get an answer.

He proved her right when he gestured toward the ring and said with gravelly pride, "Now, was that sonofagun bred for battle, or what?"

Maureen responded more to the tone of his voice than to the visual impact of the boxer's shadow falling across the canvas like a double dare. "He's tall."

"Six foot one."

Her stomach fluttered as a gloved hand flashed through the air like heat lightning. "And he's certainly got long arms."

"Seventy-seven-inch reach."

A gruesome thought occurred to her. "He doesn't take steroids, does he?"

That earned a chuckle. "He's so anti-drug, he'd give an aspirin a headache."

"Well, he's—" she faltered slightly at the sight of the naked back—"extremely well-built."

"He works out every day, rain or shine."

"I see." Michelangelo's *David*, come to life and clad in black satin trunks—that's what she saw.

"Feel his biceps if you get a chance, and you'll find he's ninety-two percent muscle."

The man's suggestion brought Maureen back to earth with a bang. She had no intention of feeling the boxer's biceps. Or any other portion of his anatomy. But her palms—those traitors!—had a mind of their own. They just itched to feel the softness of his bare flesh, the heat and steel that rippled beneath.

Clutching her purse before her with both hands, she steered the discussion to safer ground. "What's his name?"

"Jack Ryan." No sooner had she filed that away for future reference than he added, "But Sully—God rest his soul—always carded him 'The Irish Terror.' "

She'd yet to get a good look at his face, but she could just picture the cauliflower ears and flattened nose—not to mention the ugly scars—that were the inevitable result of such a violent career. To top it off, a little voice inside her said, he was probably so punch-drunk that trying to talk business with him would be a waste of both her time and her breath.

If she had an ounce of sense, she thought, she'd walk out of here now and let her lawyer handle this. Yet she stood transfixed, awed by the beauty of the beast.

The reflection of the overhead light flickered across the rippling musculature of his torso. Sweat sheened his sun-baked skin and dampened the dark pelt of hair that bisected his massive chest. Veins mapped his biceps like the road to ruin for his hapless opponents.

He was the ultimate hard body. A lean, mean fighting machine, honed to perfection by years of rigorous training.

And to think, he was all hers . . .